The Artifact

by

Maxwell Pearl

Address inquiries in permission to:
Echobird Press, echobirdpress.com
ISBN 978-1-961370-06-7 | ISBN 978-1-961370-07-4 EPUB

CHAPTER ONE

Melinda hurried through her morning chores so she could explore for the afternoon. At the moment, though, she was up to her elbows cleaning out composting toilets.

She got one half-day off from her chores every week. Unlike most girls her age, who would spend the half-day in the town center or gather together at someone's house to play games, she had always wanted to get away from everyone else and explore the area outside of town as far as she could get.

She saw her eldest sister, Kathy, talking with her mother. Her sister lived at her husband's family's house but was often back here for one thing or another. Truthfully, Melinda didn't think Kathy liked living with the Stevensons.

"Hi Kathy," Melinda waved as she grabbed the broom.

"Hi Melinda, how are you doing?"

Her mother answered before Melinda could. "She is being a stubborn child. I fear she is listening to the influence of the devil."

Kathy said, "Mother, give Melinda a break."

Melinda decided to start sweeping. It didn't make much sense to say anything. She knew Kathy would defend her.

"She spends all of her spare time *out,* somewhere. I don't even know where she goes. And she has refused to entertain the idea of marriage. She's already been asked by *three* men. Three! One of whom is the son of the priest of the town of Amos."

Melinda opened her mouth, but her sister said, "Mother, really. She does what she's told and is a help around the house, isn't she?"

"But the priest..."

"What about the priest?"

"He has said that all girls should be married by fifteen, so the devil does not tempt them. Melinda turned 15 six months ago!"

"Mother, really, just give her time. She'll be fine."

"I worry, I worry so much that she'll be..."

"She'll be what?"

"Oh, I can't talk about it. Never mind. So, you wanted some salt?"

They went into the house, and Melinda finished sweeping the porch. Her mother was constantly worried that Melinda wouldn't get married. Well, let her worry, Melinda thought.

Later, Melinda walked very quickly away from the house. She didn't look back, so if her mother called her, she could say she hadn't heard. She had her small pack, which included the pants she stole a year or so ago from her brother, a clay jar of water, some snacks, a candle lantern, her hand-drawn maps, her journal, and a couple of pencils. It was a good thing she'd finished growing - since her brother's wife was now in control of all of his clothes, stealing another pair of pants from him would be a challenge. The paper and pencils she also stole from her brother - women weren't supposed to read or write.

She was still simmering from the conversation with her mother and sister. She had no interest in marriage and the fact that it was required of her rankled. She was doing everything she could to avoid it for as long as possible, and when she could avoid it no longer, she knew she would run away. She had some ideas of where and how to run. She was the oldest girl in the village still single—except for poor Maryanne, who was too slow to have any man interested in her. Sometimes, she wished she could get away with acting that slow. She hated her life and wanted to escape it.

As she walked, the wheat in the field around her swayed in the gentle breeze - it was close to time to harvest it. Melinda reached out to a few strands of wheat and pulled them - the seeds came out in her hand. Being outside made her happy. At the end of the field was a hillock curved on three sides and a little deep, so she couldn't be seen once she climbed up and down. She dropped the bag, took out the pants, and took off her skirt. Wearing pants made her feel so much more comfortable.

Today, she thought she'd go as far to the east as possible. It was largely more small hillocks and scrub grasses, but she'd like to learn what was out this way today. She took out her map and saw where the blank space in her map started to the east. She headed in that direction, happy, at least for now.

CHAPTER TWO

Kerry paced back and forth in front of the bay where her shuttle was docked. Given the light gravity on the Moon, it was more like bouncing. From the beginning, this shipment had her stomach in a knot. The initial communications were strange, and how the negotiations went were off, somehow. But everything had checked out. McKale Simpson, the seller, and Javin Ray, the recipient of this shipment, were who they said they were and were in the business of buying and selling Terran herbs and spices.

Clicking boots approached, and Kerry turned to appraise the tall, pale man with long, flowing white hair dressed entirely in black leather.

He asked, "Kerry Jonas?"

"Yes. You must be McKale?"

"Er, no. He couldn't be here. He sent me instead. I hope it isn't a problem?"

Well, it was a problem. She frowned, her stomach twisting even more if that were possible. "Do you have the required customs forms signed by McKale?"

He answered, "Yes, I do."

She said, "Alright then. What's your name?"

"Connor McLeod."

That name rang a bell for some reason, but she couldn't place it. Well, it didn't really matter. She needed to get this done.

She finally said, "Alright, Connor. Where's the shipment?"

At that moment, two people, also dressed in black, walked in with a floating pallet between them, piled high with crates.

Connor pointed. "Here you are. Terran herbs and spices for Javin Ray, on Epsilon Eridani III."

He handed her a customs chip. "It's all here and signed by McKale."

Kerry stuck the chip in her tablet and read it. It looked in order. "Alright. Thank you." She didn't really feel it, though.

"You are welcome. Thank *you*." He inclined his head and walked serenely out of the area with his companions.

Kerry stared at them for a moment, and went to the pallet, and used the controls to direct it toward the cargo entrance. She typed in her code into the airlock, and it cranked open. She'd have to get her engineer Jeff to have a look at it – it seemed less reliable than usual. Two of her stalwart crew, Abdul and Sevy, her XO, exited to help unload.

Abdul combed back his thick, dark hair with his fingers and said, "How was the transfer?" She heard worry in his voice.

Kerry answered, "Uh. It wasn't the contact I expected, but the paperwork all seems fine. We gotta get out of here and get this cargo off our hands – it's a rush order."

Sevy, one of the more lighthearted members of the crew, smiled and said, "Well, I at least am looking forward to that little bonus you promised."

Kerry couldn't help but chuckle, and the three of them followed the pallet through the airlock directly into the cargo bay. They spent the next 20 minutes manually stacking the crates neatly in the cargo bay. When they were done, Kerry directed the pallet to go back to storage, and she closed the airlock.

She said, "Let's get out of here and get to EpYi. The faster we get rid of this shipment, the happier I'll be."

Kerry went with the others to the front of the small, 4-passenger shuttle, sat in the pilot's chair, and Abdul sat beside her. Kerry took them through the pre-launch checklist, ensuring the shuttle would get them back to their ship. They took off from the Moon with a short burst, which sank her into her seat. She didn't come to Sol system all that often, but there was always something nice about seeing Earth from the Moon. It made her smile every time.

Abdul was monitoring communications on his control board. He said, "Captain, the *John Coltrane* is ready for us."

"Thanks, Abdul."

They swung out over the Copernicus crater, and she could see the ship in the distance. The *John Coltrane* was Kerry's pride and joy. The ship was rather large for the size of her crew—she could easily have a crew twice or more the current ship's complement of nine. But the ship didn't need a crew more than that to function, so she didn't need to hire more. The fewer crew, the more profit, and the profit either went back into the ship or was shared with the crew. She wasn't one of those captains who got rich in her endeavors.

The *Coltrane* was an older ship with a large central core holding the cargo and shuttle bays, with the control center in front and the large engines in the back. Circling the central core was the spinning habitat ring, providing them with gravity for quarters, mess, and some engineering functions. It was only about 1/3 of the length of the ship. Sometimes, she wished for a newer, sleeker ship. But the *Coltrane* was powerful and got the job done, hauling as much cargo as she wanted. She could see one of the shuttle bay doors open, and the automated pilot maneuvered the shuttle into the bay. The shuttle docked. Home, finally.

Kerry turned to Abdul, the communications lead in charge of getting them out of the system. "Please get us in line for the jumpgate as soon as you can."

As he got up, he said, "Righto, Captain."

"Sevy and I will unload this cargo. Let me know when we're in line for jump."

They made their way out of the shuttle bay through the airlock. Abdul climbed toward a hub car to get up to the control room. She and Sevy stayed behind, strapping the crates together so they could pull them to the ship's large cargo hold.

Kerry said, "Sevy, something about this shipment is bothering me."

She answered, "Honestly, it's been bothering me, too. But really, Cap'n, we looked this over left and right. Up and down. We both dotted all the i's and crossed all the t's."

Kerry and Sevy finished strapping the crates together and pulled the load while they used handholds to climb to the cargo hold. Kerry said, "I know. Due diligence and all of that. But my stomach has been complaining ever since I signed the contract. If we hadn't been so desperate…"

Sevy and Kerry got the cargo to a corner of the hold and secured the load against the wall.

Sevy said, "Yeah. Well, anyway, we're a few jumps from Epsilon, probably 24 hours away. I'll be happy to see the cargo to its destination. And that bonus you promised." Kerry appreciated Sevy's sense of humor about it.

Kerry said, "Me too."

They left the cargo hold and made their way to the elevator, up to the habitat ring. Kerry made sure that her feet were positioned near the floor of the elevator, and as it moved down to the habitat ring, she could feel her weight grow. Once she reached the bottom, Kerry walked towards her quarters. She was bone tired and looking forward to shore leave once they got rid of this shipment. It had been a long five months since she'd seen Tristan.

She sat down, and looked at her tablet. She opened the customs data from Connor's chip, confirming yet again that it was all there, the requisite forms, all signed by McKale. She shook her head. Was her problem with this her own imagination? She went down the checklist for shore leave at Yagan IV, making sure that there weren't any rush or urgent shipments in their queue and making sure all of her fees due were paid up.

She sent messages to Yagan Exports and Matrix Systems, the only two companies on Yagan IV that exported anything. She also sent a message to the Yagan IV transport authority to see if there were any waiting passengers. She wasn't hopeful. Eight times out of ten, there wasn't any cargo or passengers leaving the Yagan system.

Most of her crew didn't mind doing their shore leave on Yagan or heading to a relatively close system. Yagan didn't have much to recommend it. Only a small city served the spaceport and the small backwater colony. There was little in the way of profitable cargo or passengers. If it weren't for Tristan, who was born and raised there, she was sure they'd be doing their shore leaves on some verdant paradise planet, like Hsieh V, or on Earth. She was glad her crew didn't resent her choice.

Kerry heard Abdul on the comm. "Captain, we're eighth in line for jump. Get some sleep."

"Thanks, Abdul."

Yes, sleep. That was what she needed.

She lay down on her bed, thoughts of this cargo and Tristan

zig-zagging through her mind until she fell asleep. After she woke up, she washed and went to the mess room for a meal.

Abdul was also sitting and eating his favorite turkey sandwich. "Captain, have you checked messages yet?"

Kerry said, "Um, no, I just woke up. " She went to the meal locker, grabbed a veggie burger, and put it in the heater. She sat down next to Abdul at the large central table.

He said between chews, "There is some bad news. Epsilon Eridani customs has a flag on our shipment."

She put down the veggie burger. "What?"

"Yeah." He resumed chewing.

She asked, "Why?"

He shook his head. "They didn't say. Might be one of their random flags."

Kerry groaned. "That's going to add at least 5 hours to our turn-around time."

"I know."

"Well, we'll just deal with it." She ate her veggie burger, but it was tasteless, just then.

She left the mess and made her way down to the hub and up to the control room. It was cozy but had room enough for a nice, big, comfy captain's chair. In front of her was their main pilot, Ainsley. To her left was Sevy, handling communications while Abdul was resting, and to her right, in front of his huge panel, was Gaylin, who oversaw the ship's systems.

"Status, folks."

Sevy said, "We're at Tsou, next in line for jump to Dax. I hear traffic at the Epsilon gate at Dax is light, so we should arrive at Epsilon Station Yi in about four hours."

"Thanks."

Sevy said, "You heard about the flag?"

"Indeed. I'm hoping it's random."

"Yeah. It's probably random."

Kerry settled down, watching the status messages flow through the screen before her chair. Gaylin, as usual, was quiet. Ainsley was quiet, too, and that was unusual. Her stomach wasn't quiet, and it complained the entire way through the Dax system. Just before the jump to Epsilon, Abdul came to relieve Sevy.

Kerry watched the viewscreen as they made it through the Epsilon gate.

Abdul said, "We got a message, Cap'n, marked urgent."

Kerry could feel the adrenaline begin to course through her body. "What is it?"

"They want us to stop short of EpYi. They are going to search our cargo."

That was highly unusual and clearly not a routine random flag. Kerry swore under her breath. That just slightly better-than-usual fee they had received felt rotten, and she cursed having needed it so much. It was a good thing she'd been paid already. She had no idea what kinds of fines she might be looking at.

After a few hours at the specified coordinates, their viewscreens showed a customs cruiser sidling up to their ship.

Kerry asked, "Abdul?"

"No communications yet, Captain."

"Ask them what they want us to do."

"Will do." He activated the standard customs communication channels.

"Epsilon customs agents, this is the *John Coltrane*, registry Shabazz shipyards, Captain Kerry Jonas. What are your orders, please?"

Nothing. She would try again.

"Epsilon customs agents, this is Captain Jonas; please explain this situation. We have a customer waiting for this shipment."

A disembodied voice spoke through the communications system, "No, your customer is not waiting for this shipment."

Kerry said, "Excuse me?"

"He is currently sitting in prison on Epsilon Eridani III."

"I see. Do you think this shipment is illegal? Have you examined the customs papers?"

"We know this shipment is illegal because he told us it was. It is Meadowsweet Root from Zeng Prime."

Abdul whistled. Meadowsweet Root from Zeng is one of the most sought-after hallucinogenic euphorics in the galaxy. Personal use of any drug in the galaxy was not a crime, but sales and shipment of a few drugs were illegal. Kerry futzed with the buckle keeping her in her seat – she wished there was some gravity in the control room so she could pace. She was angry at having been duped by both the seller and buyer and worried about what kind of trouble she and her crew could be in.

She said through her teeth, "We followed proper protocol, and checked out both the seller and buyer. We had no idea what it was. We will happily hand over all the cargo to you; we certainly don't want it."

"We wish to board now. Please engage your docking beacons."

Kerry turned to her systems engineer. "Gaylin?"

"Docking beacons engaged, docking lights active. They are coming in."

She realized she needed Sevy to help out with this – it was always good to have one's second around. Kerry pushed the comm button. "Sevy, meet me in the cargo bay."

"Will do, Captain."

"This is a fucking nightmare. I'm going to deal with this."

Ainsley, who was still sitting in the pilot's seat, said, "It's not your fault, Captain."

"Thanks, Ainsley. I know. But it sucks just the same."

Kerry propelled herself out of the control room using her hands and took a hub car to the cargo area. Sevy was already there.

Kerry said, "Alright, let's get this over with."

Kerry heard the docking ring engage, and Gaylin said over the comm, "The customs ship is docked, Captain; I've activated the airlock."

Four people in customs uniforms entered the cargo bay from the airlock. Because of the Epsilon system's strong androgynous culture, Kerry had no idea of their gender. They came toward Kerry.

"Hello, I'm Captain Jonas, and this is my XO, Commander delaPeña."

"I am Officer Talal Dent. You know this is a very dangerous time. We're being extra careful now. We are extraditing this shipment. The only reason we are not impounding this ship and putting you all in prison is that Mr. Ray was clear that he had misled you about this shipment. We are, however, fining you for not doing your due diligence."

Sevy said, "Excuse me? Look, we know all about the heightened security, but we did background checks on both the buyer and seller and ensured that all the right customs forms were signed properly. How is that not doing our due diligence?"

"You did not examine the interior of the shipment. That is now a requirement of all shipments coming into the Epsilon system."

Kerry countered, "First off, we hadn't heard about that new regulation – when did that go into effect? Second of all, do you know anything about the cargo business? There is the Privacy Clause, which makes us civilly liable if we examine our customers' shipments. And, if we violated the Privacy Clause, we'd have no business. It's essential to how we do things."

"Ignorance of the law is no excuse. The regulation came into effect on the first of the year. If you have a dispute, take it up with the customs court. Please indicate where the shipment is."

Kerry pointed to the corner with the stacked crates. Dent nodded. "If you'll excuse me, I have a shipment of contraband to dispose of."

They watched them take the stacks of crates out through the airlock. Kerry was trying not to fume noticeably, but she was furious. Finally, they walked out with the last crate and closed the airlock. After a little bit, they heard the sound of the airlock uncoupling.

Gaylin said on the comm, "Airlock disengaged. They're gone, Captain."

"Thanks, Gaylin. Ainsley, set our course for Yagan, please? It's time for a break. I'll be in my quarters."

She turned to Sevy. "What a fiasco! Well, they have no idea who they've been messing with. I'm not looking forward to seeing how much they decided to fine us, but I'm sure Tristan will get the money back, probably with interest! There is no way I'm going to let this one go."

Sevy said, "It's nice to know we've got talent on our side. I'm going back up to command. Why don't you get a rest, eh?"

Kerry grinned and nodded, feeling better already. She propelled herself out of the cargo bay into the small passageway alongside the outside of the cargo bay, where the hub tube was. She went to the elevator and took it up to the habitat ring, feeling the gravity slowly increase and pull her feet to the floor. She got out and walked to her quarters. Before she rested, she decided she would do a little research on this "Connor McLeod."

After searching, she found nothing. Nobody by that name could have been the man she met. Most of the Connor McLeods were either very much older than he was or very much younger. There was one Connor McLeod of the right age and relatively highly placed in the council of governors of Goethe, but when she saw his picture, she was sure he was not the same man.

She did a little more research on the people known to sell Meadowsweet Root, and she found mention of "The Gatherers," a cult which steeped itself in twencen culture, and were often involved in selling Meadowsweet Root. The more she delved into it, the more she realized they orchestrated the whole thing. She kicked herself, then revised her opinion. Yes, their attire and attitude would have been a clear tipoff, but she hadn't known of them, even though she was a fan of twencen herself.

Because that name sounded so familiar to her, she set her tablet on a random search for possible matches connected to her in some way. Out popped the fictional character of a set of twencen movies she'd loved as a teenager: "The Highlander." She had to laugh, and she had a little bit of appreciation for their abilities. From now on, she'd do a little more digging when she got that twinge in her gut.

It was a mostly uneventful trip to the Yagan system, the one big event being when they discovered that she'd been fined four times what she'd been paid for the shipment. Like most governments, Epsilon expected immediate fine payments. If she didn't pay immediately, her ship would be on the impound list, and there would be half a dozen bounty hunters after her. She paid the fine, but she had to just about empty her reserves to provide her crew with their paychecks.

There was also some good news: they were picking up several passengers at Yagan on their way to McKinney, a wealthy mining outpost. This meant that not only would they make some revenue from the passengers, but they could also pick up some lucrative cargo at McKinney.

She met Jaeden, the assistant pilot, and Gaylin at the shuttle, and they took Shuttle One to the surface, with Jaeden piloting.

Yagan IV was a very hot, dry planet, with only the far polar climes habitable by humans. Only the northern polar region was populated. It was where the colony and Yagan City were located. The southern polar region was barely explored. There was some native life, mostly rough grasses, succulents, and huge nasty bugs.

The trip to the surface of Yagan IV was always fairly uneventful; the atmosphere wasn't very turbulent, and the view was rather boring. Kerry could see Yagan City and the spaceport come into view, and the shuttle landing area became visible as they continued to descend.

The descent was smooth and easy, and they swung around the spaceport into the landing area. Finally, Jaeden nestled the shuttle into their assigned space quite neatly.

"Good driving, Jaeden."

"Thank you, Captain."

They exited the shuttle, said their goodbyes, and Kerry walked out of the dusty shuttle landing area, through the gates of the port, and into the city. Yagan IV was dry, and Kerry could already feel it in her nose. As she walked to Tristan's place, Kerry relaxed slowly. She noticed the carefully tended front gardens and could smell someone cooking something delicious.

Being with Tristan was always a pleasure, and she got to drop her leadership "persona" and just be Kerry. She liked the single city on Yagan IV. It was tiny, by Terran standards, and very sedate, with many plants and gardens. Most buildings were two and three stories high, and cute alleyways and parks were tucked away in all sorts of places. It was one of the most pleasant cities Kerry knew.

Kerry almost ran into a tall, handsome, dark-skinned young man with dreadlocks and a goatee as she turned the corner to Tristan's house.

"Oh, sorry, there," Kerry said.

The young man smiled, seeming to know who she was. "No problem. You must be Kerry. I recognize the face from pictures at Tristan's."

"I am, that. You must be Luke."

He stuck out his hand. Kerry shook it.

He said, "I'll be back for dinner. See you later."

He walked off, and Kerry made her way to Tristan's door. She stood there for under 30 seconds, and the door opened to see the smiling face of the woman she loved.

Tristan said, "Kerry, love, God, it's so good to see you!"

They embraced and went into Tristan's house. The house was the closest thing to a home that Kerry had on a planet. Some of her captain colleagues kept houses on varied colonies or on Earth if they had become wealthy, but Kerry never had. Until she'd gotten involved with Tristan, *Coltrane* was her only home, but now, she had what felt like a home here.

Tristan said, "I got your message about that scam shipment. Honey, I'm so sorry about that. We'll get the money back, you know."

Kerry dropped her bag next to the couch and sat down, feeling herself fully relaxing. Tristan joined her.

"Yeah, it was crazy. The new security protocols don't make any sense, and I don't like how the business is changing now."

"You did what you could. You always seem to bounce back. I've been hearing a lot of rumors flying around. It's unsettling."

Kerry lay down on the couch, putting her head in Tristan's lap.

"You know, I can deal with just about anything space or my

ship can manage to throw in my path. And I love my crew--I love mentoring them and love their presence with me. But people and their machinations? Spare me."

Tristan put her hand on Kerry's cheek. "Leave that to me. I'll write the appeal letter to the Epsilon customs court. You know that's my bailiwick."

"Thanks! I know that I followed all the right procedures. They had the nerve to suggest that I should have violated the Privacy Clause!"

"That's crazy. What were they thinking?"

Kerry sat upright, turning toward Tristan. "I think something really weird is happening, and everyone is getting nervous. The trade in Meadowsweet Root has been hot for years, but they usually ignore it. I have no idea how they got hold of Javin Ray. The truth is, if they hadn't, I would have delivered the shipment without having a clue. On the other hand, if Javin had not been so clear with the authorities that I didn't know what I was shipping, I'd be sitting in an Epsilon prison cell with my crew."

"And I'd have been on the next ship to Epsilon to represent you."

Kerry smiled and looked up into Tristan's face, feeling tenderness. "I remember when I couldn't imagine being with someone who wasn't a spacer. So, how are things with Luke?"

Tristan got up from the couch and turned toward Kerry. "Tough lately."

Kerry could see the worry in Tristan's eyes. "You mentioned that he has suspended all of his studies."

"Yes. He was doing quite well for a while; then, he hit some sort of emotional wall. He's a smart, sweet kid, but he had a really traumatic time at the colony, apparently. He's seeing Dr. Boomer, but he's stuck right now."

"Is he working?"

"He's got a job at the hydroponics farm at the moment. It's relatively mindless stuff, which he doesn't seem to mind. At least he's not getting into drugs like some of the banished kids do. He just seems lost and aimless."

"And that bothers you."

"It feels like a failure that I haven't gotten him onto some track in life. He'll turn 18 in three months, and he'll start living on his own. I wish I could be sure he'll be alright."

Kerry got up from the couch and put her arm around Tristan's shoulders. "You know, you can't control everything. Some people just take longer to figure things out than others do."

Tristan sighed, and they both sat back down on the couch, arm in arm.

They spent some time in companionable silence, Kerry sinking into Tristan's embrace, feeling her breathing. After a while, Kerry's stomach grumbled.

Tristan said, "Hungry, eh? I should go get a few things for dinner. Want to come?"

Kerry could feel her fatigue. "No, I'll just hang out here, if you don't mind. Settle in a little."

"That's fine. I'll be back in about a half-hour."

Tristan looked at Kerry and put a hand on her chin. "Oh, and there is a surprise waiting for you upstairs."

Kerry raised an eyebrow. "A *surprise?*"

"You'll see." Kerry and Tristan got up off the couch, and Tristan bent down over Kerry.

"You'll enjoy it..." She pitched her voice low and said quietly, "We'll enjoy it." She kissed Kerry and nibbled her ear.

Kerry grinned. She was looking forward to trying it out later.

A few weeks later, Tristan and Luke were sitting at the dining room table, where there was the evidence of a well-cooked meal strewn about. In front of Luke was the last vestiges of a piece of the birthday cake that Tristan had baked that afternoon. It had turned out surprisingly well, considering that Tristan rarely baked anything.

Luke said, "I just wanted you to know that I appreciate everything you've done for me for the past two years. I know you feel some disappointment that I haven't continued my studies."

"I worry about you, Luke. You're a smart kid--I don't want you to get stuck."

"I'll be alright, Tristan, really. I just need some time to find myself. I keep thinking about the colony, and about my child – it's so hard for me to forget that life. But I have some ideas. You don't have to worry."

Tristan frowned. She worried anyway, and she knew she would keep on worrying even now that Luke wasn't living here anymore.

"I understand. It took me a while to shake loose all of those chains in my mind from the colony. Living in the city was such a shock. I expected some sort of horrible experience. But we were all brainwashed from birth."

"I wish I could go back and tell people what life is like outside."

"Well, you know you can't. You'll get arrested, probably jailed for a long time. You know the rules."

"I know them, but I can't help wishing I could change things."

She said, to change the subject slightly, "So, do you like your new apartment?"

"I like it. It's got a nice little terrace, and it has a great view of the southern mountains. And it's good to get to live near some of my friends."

Tristan knew that Luke had befriended a group of other kids who, like him and Tristan, had been banished from the one colony on Yagan IV, the colony founded by The One True Church.

Most of the people from her generation, who had been banished fifteen years ago, where long gone from Yagan. A few, like her, stayed to help new banished kids, and she kept in touch with them, but most of the friends she'd made when she first arrived were long gone. Yagan IV didn't have anything except the colony and Yagan City, and although the city was quite pleasant, it was a backwater. No one else except the colonists and a few researchers lived outside of Yagan City. Tristan knew that at some point, her time here would be done, and she'd find somewhere else to be. She just didn't know where that was.

She realized that if she had not focused on helping new kids banished from the colony, she would probably be as lost as Luke was. She'd finished her training, become a lawyer, and worked in the colonial bureaucracy, which she had to admit wasn't all that exciting. She was a very good lawyer, but that wasn't where her heart really was. It had been the work over the last ten years helping kids from the colony find their way that had been the passion for her life.

"Well, Luke, you know you're always welcome for a good, home-cooked meal. I'd love to see you sometime, don't be a stranger, OK?"

Luke smiled. "No worries, Tristan. I'll be around."

Luke later left to go to his new apartment, and Tristan was left with an empty house for the first time in a while. Well, she knew that there was another kid who would arrive sometime soon, they always did. Five or six kids were banished each year. She'd let the citizenship office know that she had an open space.

CHAPTER THREE

It was another half-day off today, and Melinda wanted to spend some time in that cave she'd found several weeks ago. It was far enough away and tucked into the far side of a pretty tall hill. One couldn't see the entrance unless one happened upon it, which is how she found it - by complete accident. And once one went a little into the cave, it would be easy to hear anyone coming, and avoid them - there were so many nooks and crannies to hide in.

She had about an hour's walk before she got to the hill with the cave on the other side. It was so familiar to her now. The forest was bamboo, and they used it for everything. It was quite versatile. Melinda had heard her father and some men talk about how other trees couldn't grow here. She didn't know what other kinds of trees there were - she had only seen bamboo in her life.

Melinda was always curious about why they were here - a place she knew they didn't really belong. Of course, most people didn't think that. Most people felt that they did belong, that God Almighty had destined them to come to this place since they were persecuted just about everywhere else they went. Melinda knew this was a place where human beings didn't belong. She didn't quite know why she felt that, but she just did. She kept that feeling to herself. She had learned that this wasn't the planet they had originally been on. She had managed to read a bit about Earth in a small book she borrowed from her father once--a book she wasn't supposed to read.

The bamboo slowly gave way to a rough scrub. The ground was rocky, with little soil for anything much to grow. There were kinds of small bushes that sliced her hand open once, when she wasn't careful. She would sometimes sit on a rock for a long while, just noticing what was around her, and she would see the small creatures with iridescent green bodies, big eyes, and pincers she knew were sharp. One day, she'd seen a battle between one of those creatures with pincers, and a smaller, bright yellow thing with ten soft legs. She learned then that the pincers had poison - they just weren't poison to her. When the larger creature attacked the smaller one, the smaller one died before it was all that badly injured.

As she approached the hill with the cave entrance on the other side, she saw, to her dismay, two boys playing on the top of the hill, Martin and Broderick. She couldn't possibly be seen by them. Not here, and not wearing pants. She'd never seen anyone up there before. Fortunately, she could re-enter the forest and go around the hill, and approach it from the side, where there were plenty of boulders to hide her from anyone looking from above.

She stepped back into the bamboo forest, where the tall trees grew thickly, letting in only a small bit of the light of the planet's sun filtered through the green leaves. She then emerged from the forest on the other side of the hill. She kept an eye out above to make sure they weren't seeing her. She carefully made her way from boulder to boulder, then finally up the hill, hidden by an outcropping of rock. She found the entrance and went in carefully, listening for any voices. There were none. She lit her candle lantern and went further into the cave, away from the entrance.

It was a familiar place to her—she'd explored it before, and she really liked it. The dank smell and darkness didn't bother or deter her from exploring. One of her plans was to use this as a place to start her escape out into the wilds west of the village. She knew she could learn how to survive out there, even though everyone thought it was impossible. She'd bring seeds and other supplies so she could start her own farm.

There was still one part of the cave she hadn't explored, which she wanted to do today. It was a section deep inside the cave, off to the left of the caverns she'd already mapped out. She took out her map of the cave and followed it to a blank part where she hadn't drawn anything. She kept walking, and the cavern walls started to narrow some, but not too much to be worried about.

The tunnel began to descend and move in the direction Melinda knew was toward the outside, and there was a stream of water in the middle of it. She wondered whether or not the end of the tunnel led to another entrance to the cave. She made some notes on her map and kept going down, splashing as little as possible. It was a long way. She realized that since she took extra time to get to the caves, she didn't have as long to explore this time. She would have to turn around and go back, probably before finding this tunnel's end.

Melinda tripped on something. The map and candle lantern flew out of her hands, and she landed face-down in a puddle. The candle went out, and she was in pitch dark. This had happened before, so she groped around and found the lantern. The candle was wet, and she had to dry it and the lamp off before she re-lit it. The map was in the water, and as she pulled it out, it fell apart into pieces. It was a good thing she pretty much knew that map by heart--she'd have to draw it again.

She looked for what she'd tripped on. Behind her was a metal plate with a recessed handle. A metal plate? How could that be? It was a kind of metal she'd never seen before--very smooth and shiny. She pried the recessed handle up, then pulled the plate open. Just then, a part of the bottom of the tunnel where she was collapsed, and she fell, but not very far. Her candle was out again.

She scrambled to stand. There was debris all around her from the floor and walls of the tunnel. She had acquired a few bruises but hadn't been hurt. Finding her pack, she grabbed another candle. When Melinda lit it, she was awestruck. She couldn't grasp what she saw--it was completely foreign to her.

There were all sorts of... machines, she figured. She'd read about those things that the men didn't want women to read. She knew that things like this existed. But these machines were nothing like what she'd ever heard about. There were symbols and what looked like letters on them, but there weren't any letters she recognized.

It all looked very, very old--Melinda assumed that it had been covered up by that plate all these years, and the erosion from the water in the cavern floor made it much thinner and weaker than it had been before.

She saw that one area was littered with what looked like coins--about the size her father used at the market for goods. They had a large hole in the middle and were inscribed with strange symbols. They were a kind of gold color and were very beautiful and intriguing. She grabbed some of them, along with a couple of small cylindrical-shaped things and a few other small items that also had a lot of inscriptions on them. She put them in her pack and put it back on her back. It was getting late--it was time for her to make her way out.

As she turned around, she could see that her path would be treacherous. The debris was loose and threatened to make it impossible for her to get out. Melinda could feel her heart race. She had never been in this sort of situation before. She stepped carefully, slipped a few times, finally got on her hands and knees, and crawled slowly out of the cavern she'd fallen into, and back into the tunnel. But something wasn't right, she could sense the weakness of the tunnel walls as she crawled along it. She quickened her pace and tripped again, but this time, she fell to the side into the tunnel wall and the wall gave way, and a falling rock pushed her down a slope. Light came into her eyes, but she didn't understand where the light was coming from--as she rolled with the debris, she lost her bearings and couldn't tell which way was up. Eventually, she came to a stop and realized she was now outside.

She tried to move, but she fell back in excruciating pain. She looked down at her legs and saw that one leg was bent at an angle that wasn't at all right. She couldn't move her left arm, either. She had no idea how she was going to get home.

"Who's there?"

She looked to one side and saw Broderick swim into her vision. She held back an expletive. This wasn't going to be a good day.

"Melinda! What are you doing here, and... what happened?" He looked disgusted.

"I was exploring..." She didn't want to give too much away.

"Exploring? Why aren't you in town with the other girls?"

"Look, I'm hurt, and I'm going to need help. Can you help me?"

He paused and then yelled, "Martin, I need you here!"

He disappeared from her field of view, which was wavering. She was on the edge of unconsciousness. Eventually, she felt rough hands on her shoulders, and Melinda felt the worst pain she'd ever felt in her life; then, there was blackness.

Something was tapping Melinda's cheek, harder and harder.

"Melinda, Melinda, wake up!"

Her father and mother were looking at her. She didn't have the wherewithal to say anything. She looked around. She was no longer at the hill—she was in front of the priest's house, and several people besides her parents surrounded her. Shaking her head to clear it only made things worse. Her stomach roiled.

Her father said, "Melinda, the priest wants to talk with you. You must answer all of his questions."

Oh, yeah, right, she thought. She was in bad shape, but she did have enough presence of mind to know that she shouldn't do that.

"I'm injured. Can I see the doctor?"

The priest's pasty, sweaty face swam into her view. He always had bad breath, and it certainly didn't help her stomach when he opened his mouth to speak.

"Not until you answer these questions to my satisfaction, Melinda. What were you doing on that hill where the boys found you today?"

Why was he asking these questions now? Her vision blurred, and her mother asked, "Can't we get her to the doctor first? Does this need to happen now?"

The priest shouted, "Melinda, please answer the question!"

She opened her mouth to speak, and nothing came out at first. Finally, she managed to say, "I was exploring the hill and the forest."

"Do you do that a lot?"

"Sometimes."

"Don't you know that girls are not allowed to do that?"

She was silent. Nothing she said in response to that would be a good answer.

"Melinda, why do you do things you know you are allowed not to do?"

She remained silent. What *could* she say?

"This is your third offense that has been witnessed, Melinda."

She didn't even know what he was talking about. "Third?"

"Yes, Melinda. I am not going to review your sins with you. You should know them."

He turned to her father and said, "She must be banished for her sins."

Banished? She'd never heard of anyone being banished. She'd heard of some people who were there one day and gone the next. She figured they'd run away like she was planning to. But banished? She wondered what being banished actually meant.

Her mother started crying. "I knew she was going to be trouble, I knew it, Joe. I'm so sorry I couldn't help her get on the straight and narrow."

Her father said, "Satan has a hold of her and has since she was little. We cannot help her now. She's his."

She'd have rolled her eyes or laughed if she wasn't in so much pain.

She said, "Look if you are going to banish me, can you at least let me visit the doctor first?"

She heard her mother say, "Please, let her see the doctor..."

"No. She deserves none of our care! We are banishing her to the wilderness of the unbelievers. Let them treat her."

She remembered her small first aid kit in her pack. It wouldn't be much, but it might be a little helpful.

Melinda said, "Can I have my pack, please?"

The priest said, "Let's get her in the wagon—it's a long road—and get her bag."

She heard her mother say, "Let me say goodbye to Melinda, please?"

"Yes, yes, go ahead. Joe, get your wagon, please. Everyone else, it's time to go back to whatever you were doing. This is over."

She watched people leave through the hazy fog of her vision that kept fading in and out. She knew that she had been badly injured, and she didn't know exactly what was going to happen to her or where she was going.

"Melinda, look at me," her mother's face was close.

She looked to her left to see her mother next to her.

"Drink this - it will help the pain."

She drank from a cup her mother held in her hand. She could tell it contained the herb they used for pain and some others. It was bitter, but she drank it all.

"Thanks, mother."

"I am sorry it has come to this, Melinda. You knew you were in danger."

"I will be fine, mother, I will."

"How can you say that? You are about to be banished! You'll never see our family again!"

"Have you ever seen the wilderness?"

"Of course not, child! I'm sorry, so sorry." She started to cry.

Melinda said, "Mother, it's not your fault. It's me, just me. I was never meant for this place."

Her mother kept sobbing.

"You can give Felicia my clothes--she'll grow into them soon. And really, this is for the best." She knew that to really be true. To her mind, it was easier to be banished than it would have been to run away. While she didn't know what she was heading into, it could hardly be worse for her than this.

She started feeling the effects of the drink. The pain in her leg and shoulder was lessening, and she began feeling a little sleepy.

Her father said, "I got the wagon."

The priest said, "Time for us to go. Broderick, Martin, help me here."

She felt herself being lifted from the bench and into the wagon, which was a few paces away. Her father had laid a few blankets in the wagon's bed, and her pack was next to her. It was a little bit of comfort.

The priest got up into the wagon to drive it.

Her father said, "Goodbye, Melinda."

"Goodbye, father." She didn't really have anything else to say. She didn't quite know why the priest was driving the wagon, but perhaps it was because only he knew where to go. He snapped the reins, and the large, hooved animal called an aerawyn started a slow pace to start. They picked up speed, and the wagon got into a steady rhythm. Melinda fell asleep.

She was woken up by hearing voices.

She heard the priest's voice, "I have a citizen to return."

And a stranger's voice, with an odd-sounding way of talking, "Name?"

"Melinda St. John."

"Colony ID?"

There was a pause, then, "451EF221001010123."

"Alright, here's the record. Birth datetime 2325, 122.14.03?"

"Yes, that's her record."

"Reason for return?"

"Unsuitability."

"Physical, psychological, or spiritual?"

"Spiritual. Although she is also injured."

"Understood. We'll take care of her. Just a moment, I need to order the medics."

In a few minutes, Melinda was gently lifted from the wagon on the blankets by two people dressed in light blue. They put her on some kind of bed, which started to move--she couldn't imagine how it could move so smoothly without any bumps. She didn't even have time to look back at the priest. She watched the scene above her—the usual stars were washed out with a sort of glow. Then, she entered some sort of building, and the ceiling had very interesting patterns she'd never seen before.

The bed stopped moving, and a face appeared in front of her eyes.

"Hi Melinda, my name is Zair. I'm your medic tonight. Can you tell me what happened? It will help us treat you."

Her accent was strange--like the man before who had been talking with the priest. She realized she had nothing to lose in telling the truth.

"I was exploring a cave near our village, and there was a cave-in."

"Ah, I see. Alright. Do you know what was injured?"

"My left shoulder is badly injured, and my left leg."

"Yes, that looks badly broken. Anything else?"

"My head hurts, and my chest hurts when I breathe in or out."

"You likely broke some ribs. Did they treat you at all in the village?"

"My mother gave me a drink--it had some herbs I know she uses to help people in pain."

"Nothing else?"

"No, they refused."

"It's alright, Melinda. As you will soon see, we will do a much better job than they can."

Melinda would later look back on her time at the hospital and pick out things that had mystified her but made sense, like the medic holding a tablet and the varied machinery around her. But at that time, there was basically nothing for her to hold onto to help her understand what was happening. There was a lot of movement and activity around her, people talking and doing things to her. Then, she woke up somewhere completely different, and daylight was streaming into the room.

She was lying on a bed in a nondescript room. It had a window, which had a stand of bamboo trees outside. She looked around the room, and there was some recognizable furniture - a bed, a dresser, and an alcove with a sink. The dresser had her pack on top of it. She was glad to see it. She sat up and was dizzy for a moment but then felt alright. She swung her legs over the side of the bed. Her left leg looked completely normal!

She felt where she knew it had broken, and it felt a little sore but didn't hurt much. And she didn't have any sort of splint—she didn't understand how that could be.

"Well, hello! You are up."

She turned to see her medic, Zair.

"Let's see how the leg is, shall we? It was a nasty break, but the bone knitters did their job, and you should be able to stand on it just fine. Here, let me help you."

Zair offered her arms for Melinda to use as support. Melinda tentatively put her feet on the floor and started to put weight on them. They felt fine, so she kept going and stood up. She walked a few steps.

"I think I can walk."

"OK, go ahead and try. I'll be right here."

Zair let her go but hovered close. Melinda took a few steps. She felt weaker than she last remembered, but she could walk. That seemed a bit of a miracle. Her shoulder was fine, and her chest didn't hurt at all.

"How did you do this?"

"What?"

"Cure me. I would have imagined spending weeks in bed, with my leg in a splint."

"I can't explain that right now, Melinda. It's not our policy. You'll understand soon enough. You'll meet your foster parent very soon. She'll explain all of this to you."

"Foster parent?"

"She'll explain, I promise."

Melinda wasn't satisfied, but she realized she didn't have a choice.

"Are you hungry?" It was at that moment that her stomach decided to rumble loudly. Zair laughed. "I guess that's a yes. I'll be back."

Melinda walked around the room, getting used to walking, then emptied her pack on the bed. Her journal and the artifacts she'd gotten from the cave were there. Her skirt was oddly missing, as were the food and clay jar with water. Her first aid kit was gone as well. But someone had put a small pocket version of The Holiest Bible in her bag! She took it out, looking for a place to throw it.

"Don't want that anymore, eh?"

She spun around to see a tall woman in the door with dark, very short-cropped hair, wearing some of the strangest clothes Melinda had ever seen—and sporting jewelry! But she spoke a lot more like the people of her village spoke.

"No. It's not mine. Someone put it in here. I guess they thought I wanted it."

The woman grinned. "They always do that."

"What?"

"Eh, well, I'm getting ahead of myself. My name's Tristan

deSilva. I'm your foster mother. In other words, you are my responsibility for the next two years."

CHAPTER FOUR

"Jeff, have you fixed that ion stream sensor yet?" Kerry almost yelled into the comm. She was so frustrated. They should have left Salander station hours ago, and their passenger bound for Rigel was getting antsy. And they had some cargo with time pressure. This was no time for a bum ion stream sensor.

"Cap'n, I'm about two minutes away from the end of the final test set. We should be good to go in five."

It was a good thing she trusted her engineer. If he said they were leaving in five, they were leaving in five.

"Thanks, sorry I sniped."

"I understand, I do. I scared the crap out of that sensor, I did."

She laughed. Jeff was always one to personalize ship parts.

She turned to Ainsley, sitting at the navigation console a few feet away from her right arm. "Ready?"

Ainsley answered in her standard, clipped manner, "Yup."

The time readout in front of her seemed to be slowing to a crawl.

Jeff's voice blared over the comm, "Ready to go, Cap'n!"

Kerry turned toward Ainsley. "Go!"

"I've got us in line for jump – should be through in a bit."

It turned out there was a little gap in the queue, and they were up next. The passage through the jumpgate was typical, and Kerry looked forward to getting themselves to Rigel III, letting off their passengers and cargo.

Abdul said, "Captain, I have a Priority One alert! Fuck. It's the station at Rigel III."

"Priority one? What's going on?"

"The colony at Rigel III is under attack by unknown forces... Oh, no! Signals from the station have stopped, dead. I'm hearing multiple distress calls from all over the system."

"What the hell...?"

Abdul said, "There's a lot of crazy chatter, Captain. This looks really bad."

"What could be happening?"

"There's gotta be a war going on."

Kerry said, "Let's get the hell out of here before we get involved."

"Captain, unknown ships are heading this way and shooting at other ships as they pass!"

"Ainsley?"

"Yes, Captain, we're jumping!"

Once they got back to the Salander system, things were chaotic. There was a long queue of ships waiting to jump to Rigel, and it looked like a lot of ships just barely made it out, like them.

Abdul said, "I'm hearing the Jump gate isn't working anymore."

"Isn't working?"

"That means it was destroyed on the other side."

Kerry realized then that the ships hadn't come from here. The Rigel system was one of those odd ones with only one jump gate, which led to the Salander system. So where had they come from? And no one had bothered to attack a human colony in how long? It had been at least a hundred years since the Zoar War. It was frightening.

Kerry said, "Damn. Alright. I gotta talk with our guest – he might be glad he missed the drama."

She unstrapped from her chair and held the back of it while she swung around toward the door to the control room behind her. She grabbed a tablet from the cubby by the door and went aft to a tube that would take her to the habitat ring. She stepped on the platform which then quickly dropped her down to the habitat ring, and she could feel the increasing weight as she went. At the bottom, she walked aft and around to the quarters where her passenger stayed. She knocked.

A voice said, "Come in."

She slid the door open and saw him poring over some papers. Yes, he missed the drama.

"I have some bad news."

He looked up. "Oh, no, is your ship still broken?"

"No, I wish it were that. We jumped to Rigel, then had to jump right back. Someone unknown was attacking Rigel – they probably destroyed the station and the jumpgate. Here's some details and the new alert that's going out everywhere."

She handed him the tablet.

He spent some time reading and then said quietly, "I see."

"You don't seem surprised." Kerry didn't quite understand his reaction.

He shook his head. "No, I'm not. I was predicting it."

She didn't like this mystery, not at all. "You know what this is about?"

"Yes, unfortunately, I do. I was going to Rigel to warn them. I guess I was too late. At least your broken ship clearly saved all of our lives. If we had gotten to Rigel earlier, we likely would have been destroyed along with the station."

"But what do you think happened on Rigel? Want to let me in on this?"

He shook his head. "I imagine the worst, Captain. And I'm sorry, I can't. Galactic Central..."

Kerry was worried, sad, and angry all at once. "Security, yadda, yadda. Alright then. What a horrible mess. I had some friends on Rigel. I hope they made it out. Anyway, I have some cargo for which I'll need to find a home. Do you have a new destination?"

"Epsilon Station Yi. I need to talk with anyone who might have witnessed anything."

"We're already on our way there. That's a pretty likely home for our cargo in any event. "

"Thank you, Captain."

"You are welcome, Dr. Greenwald, although I don't very much like the news you carry."

She walked out and closed the door behind her. He was a mystery, that man. He had been a passenger on her ship several times, and they got along well, but she didn't really know that much about him. She knew he was an archeologist specializing in ancient alien civilizations, especially the ones that were extinct in the galaxy. Why would an archeologist who specialized in extinct species predict invasions? She shook her head. And then she remembered Stevie and Jane. And then she had to break herself out of the morose mood. She had work to do. It was her job to take care of her ship and crew, and that she would. She went up to her quarters, sat at her desk, and started to make contacts and see who might want the shipment of Gilaurian glass vases that the buyer on Rigel had been so desperate for but now was probably not caring much about one way or another. There might be a buyer on Epsilon, but even if she couldn't unload them there, she still had some cargo space and could pick up Eridani IV Ice Wine - she could always sell that almost anywhere, at a very sweet profit, as sweet as the wine itself.

She turned on the comm at her desk. "Ainsley, we're going to Epsilon Eridani."

"Course already set, Cap'n. It's four jumps from here. Depending on traffic, we should be there in about 20 hours."

"Gaylin, systems ready?"

"All systems are go. The routines are set, and the jumpgate API is loaded. We're ready."

"Let's get the hell out of here, shall we?"

Ainsley said, "Yes, Cap'n." Kerry could hear the sadness in Ainsley's voice.

Kerry could sense the small changes in the sound of the ship as it accelerated away from the station and toward the jumpgate. She looked at her display - they were fourth in line. She'd better get up to the bridge.

As she settled back in her seat on the bridge and strapped in, she wondered what they would find at Epsilon. Epsilon had two habitable planets that were very crowded, and a few stations. Rigel didn't have a large population because Rigel III, the only habitable planet in the system for humans, wasn't the nicest of places. It has a very dry climate, rocky, with not a lot of native vegetation, and not a lot of food crops could grow there. They had several interesting colonies, but not of the very standard types. It reminded her of Yagan IV, where Tristan grew up. Her mind wandered to think of Tristan for a moment, but she shut down that train of thought--that would not help her now to worry about Yagan IV.

She figured that the main station at Epsilon was going to be chaotic--she'd suggest that most of the crew stay aboard the ship. She'd put an ad in Merchant Central for the Gilaurian glass vases and hoped she'd have a bite by the time she arrived in the system. She'd already reserved forty cases of the ice wine.

She sighed. This was going to be a mess, and she was glad it wasn't her job to deal with it. There hadn't been a war in her lifetime--all she knew about war she'd studied in school. At one time, humans were always at each other's throats on Earth, but after First Contact, humans realized how big the galaxy was and how small and petty human conflicts on Earth were. It took several decades, but finally, humans got more interested in spreading out across the galaxy than fighting back on Earth.

Once species in the galaxy got to know each other, there had always been a conflict or two around this system or that one. Terrans got into only one of those fights because they had chosen to settle on a planet that had been claimed by the Zoar, who were an insectoid species that lived on the far side of the galaxy. Terrans hadn't known that, and the Zoar demanded that the Terrans leave, but they refused. The Zoar invaded the colony, and Terrans were determined to defend their right to the colony. But they were in the wrong and eventually surrendered the colony. It had been a nasty fight and a tough defeat. But that was over 100 years ago. Terrans didn't build much in the way of weapons systems anymore—humans were so far down the technological ladder that it wasn't worth it.

Mostly, the two dozen or so galactic species got along fairly well. Most species were less war-like than humans, and there were some ongoing scuffles among the most war-like, but they didn't involve humans and were generally at some distance from where most Terran colonies were. The jump-gate system, put in place by a species that no one knew much about because they kept to themselves, was used by all the species, and there hadn't been many disputes over territories in a long time. She couldn't understand what would cause a species to attack Rigel, a system that humans had been occupying for more than two hundred years. It was one of the first colony worlds, even though it wasn't especially hospitable. But it was a place where many offbeat colonies got their start.

And the strange thing was how did they actually get to Rigel to invade, if it weren't via Salander? It was a mystery to her, but she wasn't going to learn much more about it until they got to Epsilon Station Yi, or EpYi as most spacers called it. She shook her head and started to pay more attention to business. She'd posted passenger availabilities just a few minutes ago, and there were already four people who wanted to come aboard, even if it would take a while to get to their destinations. They were all refugees from Rigel.

Ainsely said sourly, "Cap'n, what do you think of all this?"

Kerry turned to Ainsley, who had stirred her out of her deep consideration of what it would mean to have a lot of passengers.

"You got me, Ainsley. Dr. Greenwald says that the reason he was on his way to Rigel was to warn them because he'd predicted this, but he wouldn't tell me any more about it. I can't quite figure out why someone like him would be doing this sort of thing."

"Yeah, isn't he an archeologist?"

"Yup."

"My dad did that. All he did was spend time in dusty old caverns in far-flung places, mostly where he had to wear a suit, and piece together the stories of artifacts that were sometimes millions of years old. It was kinda cool to hear the stories, but it seems a far stretch to predicting alien invasions."

Kerry nodded. "I don't get it, and he isn't saying, so I guess it will remain a mystery to us for the time being."

"I know you're going to suggest that most of us stay ship-side when we get to EpYi."

"Yes, I'm sure it's going to be a madhouse with all of the refugees and such. I think it's best most of you stay. I've got to get Dr. Greenwald situated, make sure our Eridani wine gets delivered to our bay, and find a buyer, hopefully, for the vases. I also need to check in with the customs office about that contraband shipment problem we had a few months ago.

"Anyway, why?"

"Well, my ex Peter is living at EpYi now, and I'd like to go see him and make sure he's OK."

"Alright--I understand. If there is danger, I don't want to have to go hunting for my crew."

"Understood. I'll be careful and won't dilly-dally."

"We probably should stay for less than 24 hours. I should have a buyer for the ice wine soon, so we'll know where we're heading. And we already have four passengers coming on board at EpYi, and I expect a full load."

"Twelve passengers? I don't think we've had twelve passengers since..."

"I know, don't remind me."

"You said you'd never take a full load again, as I recall."

"Well, this seems like extenuating circumstances. All four passengers so far are refugees from Rigel, and I imagine the rest will be as well, or at least trying to get as far away from here as they can."

Ainsley nodded. Abdul said, "I'm happy to stay here. I have several good sims to get through. And I'm sure Jeff will be happy working on whatever needs work. There is always something that needs work. I feel for him."

Ainsley said, "He loves it, Abdul, don't worry about him."

Kerry smiled. Yes, if anyone loved his job, it was Jeff. She was grateful to have such a good engineer. She remembered when he was wet behind the ears and just starting out. For some reason, she'd had a lot of faith in him, even though there wasn't much evidence for it. He ruined a few parts at first, but he turned out to be the best engineer she knew.

She thought that just about all of her crew were the best she knew. She'd gotten them all before they'd proved anything, and some people said she should take credit for their successes, but she just thought she was doing a little to nurture them, and they did all the hard work of it.

The control door opened, and Kerry saw the tall, bulky form of Sevy, her XO, enter the control room.

"Abdul, I'm here--your turn to sleep, bud."

"Ah, thanks Sevy. You're a lifesaver."

Sevy took Abdul's place at the communications console, and he left the control room.

"Captain, I hate to say it, but you look exhausted. Go get some shuteye."

Sevy was probably the only crew member who could order the captain around. It probably was because she had been on this ship for almost as long as Kerry had.

"Good idea, friend. I'm off to bed. You know when to wake me."

Sevy nodded, and Kerry launched herself from her chair and went out to the habitat ring to her quarters. She was exhausted and hungry, but more exhausted than hungry, so food would wait until the morning.

She hadn't really gotten a good night's sleep, but at least she got a solid breakfast. It was a good thing, because the minute they entered the Epsilon system, chaos reigned. Abdul was busy fielding tens of calls from people looking for transport away because everyone was afraid that Epsilon was next. They'd already taken their twelfth passenger before they even got to Epsilon. And no one had wanted the Gilaurian vases--everyone in the Epsilon system was on edge and more interested in leaving if they possibly could. It was putting everyone on the ship on edge.

They approached EpYi slowly, and Kerry could see that the docking areas were completely full and that tens of ships were orbiting around the station.

"Abdul, can we get docking clearance?"

He shook his head, "I haven't had any luck so far, Captain."

She pushed some icons to get Dr. Greenwald on the com.

"Dr. Greenwald?"

After a pause, she heard, "Yes, Captain?"

"We can't seem to get docking clearance at Epsilon Station Yi. Can you help?"

"Certainly, just a moment."

In about five minutes, Abdul said, "Captain, we have docking clearance, but not for the ship, for a shuttle."

She sighed. The shuttle would have to make five trips to bring all of the Eridani wine on board.

"Alright. Fine. Tell them we'll be there in an hour."

She raised Dr. Greenwald again, "Thank you. We have shuttle docking clearance. Please meet me in the shuttle area as soon as possible."

"Will do."

"Ainsley, coming?"

"Aye, Captain."

She unstrapped and pushed herself out of her chair, grabbed a tablet, and left the control room with Ainsley. They got into one of the small hub transport cars and were in the shuttle launching area in a few minutes.

A voice next to her said, "Captain."

She turned to see a second hub car arrive next to theirs.

"Dr. Greenwald, we're taking Shuttle One. It's the largest we've got, and I've got a lot of ice wine to bring back. It's going to take several trips."

"Sorry I couldn't get your ship clearance. There are too many ships coming in from Rigel, let alone the ships that were bound for Rigel that ended up here."

"It's alright; I appreciate what you've done. Shall we?"

She pointed the way to the shuttle, and they made their way via handholds to the entrance. She keyed in the code to enter the shuttle, and the door opened.

"The passenger seats are back there, Dr. Greenwald."

"Thank you."

She and Ainsley prepared for launch.

"Gaylin, open shuttle doors, please."

"Yes, Captain."

The doors opened in front of her, and the station and ships milling about could be seen ahead. They would have to be careful. They slowly launched.

"Abdul, Gaylin, docking beacons?"

"Fucking shit!" That sounded like Abdul's voice to Kerry.

"What's going on?"

Abdul said, "They haven't gotten their act together yet. Just a second, I've sent another request."

She turned to Ainsley and said, "I have a feeling this is not going to be fun. Not at all."

"I concur."

Finally, Abdul's voice came back over the comm, "Gaylin, are you seeing the beacons?"

"Yup, I got 'em. Docking beacons engaged, Captain."

She breathed a sigh of relief as they let the autopilot follow the beacons in. It was a slow trip—because of the number of other ships, the autopilot was being especially careful.

Ainsley said, "I don't think I've seen so many ships at one station before."

"I don't think I have either."

The rest of their trip to the station was without incident, but Kerry was pretty sure that she was not going to be able to make five trips with wine back to the ship. She would most likely have to make do with whatever she could fit in this shuttle on their trip back.

They docked, exited the top airlock, and took the docking elevator to the first level of the station. Once they left the very small embarking area for their dock, they entered complete chaos. People lay in the halls, ran to and fro, and crowded the spaces.

"Dr. Greenwald, I guess I shouldn't be sorry we couldn't get you to your destination, but, well, you know..."

"I understand. I do hope I get to fly with you again sometime."

"Well, you're a great passenger each time we've had you. Stay safe until next time, OK?"

He nodded, "You too – I can't say much, but I'm sure there's more coming. Be careful."

He then headed away. She assumed he knew where he was going, and she turned to her crew member.

"Ainsley, meet back here in four hours. I don't think we'll get to make more than one trip."

"Righto. See you later."

Kerry's first visit was to the customs office to straighten out that old issue, and as she approached the office, she could see that there was no point in bothering. The line to the customs office was snaking down three corridors, and although it didn't make sense to her, it must have been related to Rigel. She'd have to deal with it next time she was here.

It was that shipment of what she had been told was Terran herbs and spices but turned out to be an herb from Zeng Prime that was an illegal substance. She was fined heavily for "not doing her due diligence" and was lucky they hadn't impounded her ship. She *had* done her due diligence but had been duped anyway, and she and Tristan had been fighting the fine in customs court for months. Finally, one judge ruled in her favor, and she had a bit of paperwork to sign to get refunded most of the fine.

But today was not the day she was going to get satisfaction on this matter. She turned and went toward the marketplace to get her Eridani wine.

In the end, she'd been right—one trip, and one trip only. After three hours, they'd threatened to unlock the docking ring unless she left immediately. She'd messaged Ainsley, who was back at the dock very quickly. They piled as much ice wine in every corner of the shuttle as they could--there were even several cases sitting between the pilot and co-pilot's chairs. Their passengers were all present and accounted for. They took off and went back to the *John Coltrane*. She'd found a buyer on Goethe II that wanted the vases. They had a full complement of paying passengers, so they wouldn't end up doing too badly today, even with the Rigel disaster. She was curious about what happened at Rigel and how bad it was—she imagined her passengers would have some things to say about it.

When the *Coltrane* had finally left the system—they had been an unprecedented thirtieth in line for the jump gate to Behrend—Kerry,

Ainsley, Liana, and Sevy were eating with some of the passengers in the mess. One of them had been on a shuttle on the way to an outpost on Rigel V, and the rest had been at Rigel station and had managed to get on a ship about to leave when the attack came.

One said, "Man, it was crazy. I was in the shuttle, and we were swinging by Europa, Rigel III's moon, and we saw all of these ships coming out of nowhere toward Rigel III. Tons of them. And they started to shoot at any ships they came across. The pilot of the shuttle was sharp - he just turned right around and headed as fast as he could to the jumpgate. We hitched a ride on the second ship out."

Kerry said, "Yeah, we could tell the ships weren't coming from the gate."

"No, they weren't! Can't say where they were coming from."

No one else had seen much--Rigel station had been in chaos, and they were very lucky to get on a ship before the station itself was attacked. Kerry knew that it had been many hours since any ships came from Rigel, and she'd heard it confirmed that the Rigel jumpgate had been destroyed. It didn't surprise her. If some aliens had come to destroy a colony, they certainly didn't want anyone coming through the gate, especially since they didn't need it. But it didn't make her happy to hear that thousands of people were either dead or stuck with hostile aliens on a planet without a jump gate.

They made it to Goethe without incident, and Kerry thought it was about time she went back to Yagan's quiet. She wondered what poor waif Tristan was fostering now.

CHAPTER FIVE

Melinda followed Tristan closely, as they left what she had called "hospital."

"Melinda, there is a lot that is going to confuse you. Just walk right near me. I promise nothing will hurt you."

Melinda had been given new clothes: a comfortable, loose pair of pants and a shirt that looked similar to the one Tristan wore—with patterns, buttons going diagonally down the front, and odd, pointed collars. It was nothing like the shirts that anyone wore at home.

Tristan had said, "You can choose whatever clothes you like later; these are just for now. It will take time for you to get used to what we wear and figure out what you like."

"I like these fine," she'd said. She really did.

"OK, well, you can keep them, and we can get more like them."

Melinda looked around as they walked. She saw a lot of people and carts and wagons that looked very strange and went far too fast for her to understand. Some were small enough that only one person could fit in, but others were so large that they carried tens of people.

They walked down several streets, then turned corners, and kept walking. Tristan stopped at one point on a quiet street with only a few people.

She said, "OK, this is the place. You won't need to know this for a while, but it would be good to remember. We live at 452B Wellfleet Street, Zone Four. Can you remember that?"

"452B Wellfleet Street, Zone Four."

"Good. If you get lost, ask anyone for that, and you can get home."

She said it internally in her head a few times. Her village had streets, so she was familiar with the idea of a street, but none of the houses had numbers on them.

"What's a zone?"

"It's just a section of the city."

"City? Is this where we are, a city? I've read about them... well, not really. Just read about how they are supposed to be horrible places. The centers of the wilderness of the unbelievers."

Tristan laughed. "I'm glad to hear you got to read. Most girls that come out can't."

"My mother had learned to read, and she taught me. I guess she thought I'd use it for recipes or something. But I used to sneak books from my father's library to read."

"Good for you."

Melinda looked at the building. It had two stories and seemed to be made of some sort of smooth stone, very different from the houses that they had in the village, which were a combination of bricks and bamboo. Tristan put her hands onto some sort of symbols on the side of the door, and it opened for her. They entered a large room that Melinda could understand. There was a couch and chairs—like her family's living room.

"Come on in. Let me first show you to your room. You'll want to orient yourself there, then I can show you the house. Some of it will be a little... well, a little confusing at first."

Tristan walked up the set of stairs tucked into the side of the first room they'd entered. At the top of the stairs was an open door to a large room with a very large bed and some other furniture.

"This is my room—feel free to knock whenever, I mean it-- *whenever* you need. Even the middle of the night."

Melinda nodded.

Tristan pointed to the next door, which she opened. "Here's your room."

It was a simple room but much larger than the one she'd shared with her sisters. It had a large bed, a desk, and a dresser.

Tristan opened one of the doors inside the room.

"Here's the closet, which also leads to the bathroom."

Melinda now knew about bathrooms in this place—wonderful, luxurious things that were easy to use and had a seemingly unlimited supply of hot running water. In the hospital, she had spent a very long time in the shower, waiting for the hot water to run out. Her fingers were so wrinkly when she decided that it wouldn't.

"Why don't you just get acquainted with this room and settle in? Dinner will be in about two hours, and I'll give you a full tour of the place then.

"Thanks."

Tristan left and closed the door behind her. Melinda went to the window, which looked out onto a courtyard full of bamboo and pots of flowers. This seemed a very lovely place. Hardly the "wilderness of the unbelievers" that had been described to her many times.

She spent a while exploring her room and enjoying more of the unlimited hot water. As it got dark outside, she realized there weren't any lamps. Checking down the hall, she saw that Tristan wasn't in her room. There was light downstairs, but from where? She went downstairs to ask Tristan.

"Tristan, do you have any lamps?"

"We don't need lamps, Melinda. Everything is controlled by what we call a house 'system'. Did your priest have a servant?"

"Yes, he had five."

"Wow, I guess he was one of the more important ones. Anyway, think of this system as a servant. It's just named 'House,' and you can ask it questions or ask it to do things. If you go upstairs and say, 'House, turn on the lights in this room,' the lights will come on. You can also ask it to make the lights dimmer or brighter."

"Does it do anything else except control the lights?"

"Yes, Melinda, it does many things, but they won't make much sense to you for a while. You'll learn about it over time."

"OK, I'll try it."

She returned to her room and said, "House, turn on the lights in this room." The room became way too bright.

"House, please dim a little." The lights dimmed to a more comfortable level.

She wished there were some books in her room. She'd have to ask Tristan about that--so far, she hadn't seen any books at all. Maybe Tristan didn't like to read.

She sat on her bed, thinking about everything she'd seen. It was pleasant; people were friendly to her and gave her what she needed. Someone taking care of her who seemed to be a decent person— nothing like the priest. Why were people afraid of this?

She heard a light, melodic voice say, "Melinda, dinner is ready." Her door was closed, and there wasn't anyone in the room, yet she'd heard the voice. She wondered if it were "House."

"House, is that you? You can speak?"

"Yes, Melinda, I can speak."

"How do you speak?"

"There is a recessed speaker in the ceiling."

"Speaker?"

"An electronic device to create sound."

"Electronic?"

There was a pause, then, "Tristan wishes you to go down to dinner, Melinda. She says you'll learn all about it soon enough."

She got up from her bed, and walked downstairs, through the living room, to a room with a table and chairs. It was set with two places, and there was food on the table. Tristan entered the room from another that Melinda couldn't see much of. Perhaps it was the kitchen.

"House tells me you've been curious about how it can speak."

"Yes, it's very interesting."

"There's a lot more to learn, but now it's time to eat, OK? I made a meal that I hope will be familiar enough for you. The food you are used to is quite different than the food we have here."

"Why is that?"

"We don't depend just on crops that can grow in the native soil or animals that can be raised here. We have large hydroponic farms that can grow just about anything from Earth, and then we get lots of imports from all over..."

Melinda was confused, and she could tell Tristan could see it.

"Let's eat. There's a lot for you to learn, yet."

Melinda sat down and saw some familiar things. A loaf of bread, some tato root mash, and what looked like aerawyn roast. But then there were unfamiliar green things and sliced rounds of something red with seeds. She waited for Tristan to start. Tristan handed her a plate full of the roast. At home, as the second-youngest daughter, she'd be second to last served and might not get everything since there wasn't always enough. But here, it looked like there was plenty of food for both of them.

"Mmmm, this is so delicious. I've never had aerawyn roast

made like that. And the mash! These round red things…"

"They are called tomatoes."

"I've never tasted anything like them."

"They can't grow here natively, but we grow them in the hydroponics farms."

"Hydroponics?"

"It's a way to grow food in water without the need for soil. It's used a lot because the soil here is very difficult. Anyway, most of the vegetables we eat here are grown this way. You'll get a tour of the farms."

Melinda was curious. "I will?"

"Yes, it's part of your education."

She was now more surprised than curious. "I'm going to be educated?"

"Yes, Melinda. Here, every child, boy or girl, is educated. They can get as much education as they want. The later part of that education is to learn about what kinds of things they might want to do in their lives."

"Do? Like as in being a medic or something?"

"Exactly."

Melinda put her fork down. "What is it that girls are allowed to do?"

Tristan looked up from her plate. "Anything boys are."

"How can that be?"

"Melinda, it's the way the galaxy works. Think of it this way: you were in a place you thought was the entire world. And you knew there was more, but it was undefined, and maybe even scary, because the adults wanted it to be scary. The truth is, you were in a very small colony on a small planet in one corner of the galaxy. There are thousands of Terran colonies in the galaxy. Everything outside your world is a much bigger place than you'd ever been taught."

Melinda let out the breath she was holding. "Terran?"

"Yes, human. From Earth. Earth is our home planet, the place we started from."

"The place God cast us out from?"

Tristan smiled. "Er, no. No one cast us out. You can go there if you want—you are a Terran galactic citizen and have the right to visit whenever you want."

"I can visit Earth? But..."

"Melinda, your family, and all of the families in that colony, including mine, live a lie. They are not the chosen people; they were not banished from Earth by God, and they are just one of a couple dozen or so fundamentalist religious sects that have colonies around the galaxy."

"You grew up in my village?"

"No, it was a couple of villages away. But I grew up the way you did and was banished as you were fifteen years ago. At least for now, I make it my work to help kids who are like I was figure out what's next after that."

Melinda didn't know what to say. She couldn't have imagined that the world was like this. She felt that she had so much to learn. Too much. She looked at Tristan, who had an apologetic look on her face.

"So, tomorrow, you need to be assessed."

"Assessed?"

"Yes, it's standard. To figure out how best to educate you, we need to know your aptitude for various things and your knowledge base. It will be a long and probably bewildering day for you. But it's important and necessary."

"Alright. I can handle it. I want to get started."

Tristan smiled. "Why am I not surprised?"

After dinner, Tristan and Melinda sat in the living room and talked about Melinda's family.

Melinda said, "I have a brother and three sisters. My brother and two sisters are older, and I have one younger sister. She's 13. My brother and his wife live in our house, and my two older sisters live in their husbands' houses. They both got married at 14. I knew I never wanted to marry and knew I'd have to run away to avoid it."

"They didn't tell you you'd be banished if you refused to marry?"

"No, they never did. If they had, I'd just have agreed to be banished. It might be my mother—I remember hearing that her sister had disappeared mysteriously, and she told my older sister she worried that something would happen to me that she refused to talk about. I wonder if her sister had been banished, and my mother wanted to ensure I didn't end up that way."

"Well, that whole colony has about forty thousand members, and they banish about five kids yearly."

"That many?"

"Yes, that many. About a dozen of us help the kids, although not all of us were born in that colony. Most people who are banished end up leaving the system entirely. I know I will someday, but I do not seem quite ready yet."

"What was your family like?"

"Much like yours. I was the only daughter, and I had three older brothers, so it was a very big house with their wives joining us. I used my half-day off to get as far from the village as possible. There was a nice clearing in a bamboo forest in which I used to spend time."

"You liked to explore, too?"

"Yup."

"Was that why you got banished?"

Tristan laughed. "No. I got banished because I got caught kissing one of my brother's wives."

Melinda smiled. "I think that was one of the sins they counted against me. I got caught with a friend with our shirts off."

"What happened to her?"

"She got scared and was married the next week. She never wanted to see me again."

"Well, Melinda, just so you know..."

"What?"

"There isn't anything wrong with that. We don't think it's a sin, or wrong, or anything. Things are just more... more fluid than you've been taught."

Melinda nodded. It seemed to fit with everything else she was learning about this place... about everything.

"OK, kiddo, you have a big day tomorrow. I think it's time that you got some sleep."

Melinda started to get up but then stopped. "I have one question before I go to bed."

Tristan looked up at her. "What is it?"

"Where are the books? It would be nice to have a book to read right now."

Tristan got up, opened a drawer, and took out an odd-looking rectangular translucent object. She handed it to Melinda.

"This is just about every book that was ever printed, Melinda. The Holiest Bible is even in here."

Melinda held the device carefully. "How is that possible?"

"I can't explain it in a way you'll understand now. But you will later. Anyway, there is a small, recessed button here..." Tristan pointed to one side, and Melinda pushed it, and the glass lit up with a list of books.

"Those are just some books I thought you might want to start with. History, and such. Just tap the place where the title is…"

Melinda saw the title "A Short History of Yagan IV." She'd already heard at some point that was the name of the planet they were on. She tapped it, and paragraphs of text came up.

"To go to the next page, just swipe from right to left, like you were turning a page. To go back, do the reverse. To get a table of contents, or search, tap the top, and a little menu will appear."

"Thank you! This is amazing! All the books?"

"Yes. You can use House to control it. You can ask House to search for a book and put it on this tablet."

"Thank you! Good night, Tristan."

"Good night, Melinda, don't stay up too late reading. You'll need your rest."

Melinda nodded and went upstairs.

"Melinda, it is time to get up." The melodic sound of House's voice woke her, and she could see the sun streaming in from the window.

"OK, House, I'm getting up."

"You have approximately one and one-half hours before leaving for your assessment."

She got up, took a nice long shower, and went downstairs, where Tristan had laid out breakfast.

"I figured I'd make you a hearty breakfast. Eggs, potatoes, the works."

"Wow, I haven't had eggs in a long time."

"Really? We used to have eggs almost every day when I was a kid."

Melinda sat down at the table. "We only have a few chickens, and there aren't enough eggs for everyone. So, I rarely got any."

"Well, this little block has a collective coop with about twenty chickens. We can get eggs whenever we want."

Melinda scooped potatoes from the dish onto her plate. "Do other blocks have coops?"

"Yes, most do."

After finishing breakfast, House said, "It is time to leave for the assessment appointment."

Tristan said, "Thank you, House."

Melinda asked, "Are people generally polite to their systems?"

"It seems so. I learned that."

Melinda laughed, remembering. "The priest isn't very polite to his servants."

"Not a very nice priest, eh?"

"No, he was horrible."

Tristan opened the door for Melinda. "Well, the system won't care whether you are polite or rude, but most people are polite."

They left the house and walked a few blocks. Melinda still hadn't gotten used to the streets and the vehicles on the streets that were going so fast. Even though she'd seen everything yesterday, it was still new to her.

Tristan seemed to tell that she was ill at ease and put her hand on her shoulder. "You'll get used to it, Melinda."

They arrived at a building taller than most, with more glass in the front than Melinda had ever seen. The building was angular and sharp, and she could see people doing things inside.

Tristan said, "Here we are."

"What is this building?"

"It's a sort of administration building. The person taking the assessment today has his office here."

Melinda was nervous to go into the building, but she followed Tristan. They went inside and walked toward the back of the building, where there were sets of glass stairs. They climbed many stairs and then walked on a bridge that was suspended in the middle of the building. Melinda could see up and down. It was pretty scary—Melinda was sure she'd never been this high up in her life. And as she looked up, she could see the sky. They crossed the bridge, walked down a long hallway, and finally entered a large room where a man sat at a desk.

As he got up, she could see that he was quite tall, with a bit of a paunch. He had skin a similar color to Melinda's. He had very short hair and a goatee.

He came to them. "Tristan, hello! And this must be Melinda. Welcome. Please, Melinda, sit here." He pointed to the chair across from where he was sitting. He got up and went toward Tristan.

Tristan hugged him and said quietly, "I think you'll find this one quite interesting."

He smiled, the small wrinkles on the sides of his eyes crinkling. "Alright. With that introduction, I'm quite looking forward to it. I have lunch for her, so you can just come by around four to pick her up."

Tristan nodded and said loudly, "See you later, Melinda."

Melinda sat and watched the man come back to the desk.

"Hi Melinda, my name is Josh Wyndam, and I'm here to give you some tests. Some of it is going to be interesting, and some of it is going to be long and boring. Just a warning."

She nodded. "OK, I'm ready."

The desk in front of her came alive, and she jumped back.

"Sorry, I always forget to warn some people of that."

"It's OK; I'm sort of getting used to being surprised now."

"There are several things we're testing for today. Certain kinds of aptitudes, like for math or language, things like that. And we'll be testing a bit for knowledge, so that we have a baseline. There's also a bit of psychological assessment here."

"Psychological? I remember that word - the guard at the gate had asked that about me."

"It's a standard question for people returning from colonies. It's just about your state of mind."

"Alright. Can we get started?"

Josh smiled. "Of course. You'll see a question in front of you, with some possible answers. Just tap the answer that you think is most right. There is no penalty for guessing, so please, if you aren't sure about the answer, just guess. If you have any questions, just ask."

The first question on the desk was an easy one. "If an aerawyn can go four kilometers an hour, and you must travel seven kilometers, how long will that take?"

The questions got increasingly complex, but she could answer all of them fairly easily. Then there was a question that made absolutely no sense to her.

She asked Josh, "What's a shuttle?"

"Pretend it's a cart."

"But a cart can't go that far."

"Pretend it can."

She kept going with the questions pretending things were things that she understood, but clearly they could do things that were impossible. She then got to a list of questions that were just definitions of words. She didn't know most of them. Some were words she'd heard, like "electronic" but she had no idea what they meant.

After a while, Josh said, "Are you getting hungry? It's been a few hours. I think it's time for a break for lunch, yes?"

"That sounds great--I'm definitely hungry."

Josh took out a bag, where there were a couple of sandwiches, and two strange-looking cylinders.

"Lemon or grape soda?"

"What is 'lemon' and 'grape'?"

"OK, do you like sweet or tart?"

"Sweet."

He handed her one of the sandwiches and opened one of the cylinders--it was purple on the outside and handed it to her. She took a few sips.

"Wow, this is really nice tasting. I've never tasted anything this sweet before."

"I imagine you don't get much sugar."

She shook her head. "Only on very, very special occasions. It's one thing that appears, and no one asks questions about it."

"That, and I expect the powder for that sour drink everyone has to drink once a week or so?"

"How did you know?"

"One of the things I do, besides doing these kinds of assessments, is to work with others to keep tabs on how the colonies are going and make sure that you are getting things you need. The powder is called 'Vitamin C,' and if we didn't send it to you, and you all didn't use it, you would die of something called 'scurvy' since there are no natural sources of that vitamin on Yagan IV.

So all of this was just under her nose her whole life, but no one acknowledged it or told any of us about it. Well, she amended, didn't tell any of the women. She imagined many of the men knew, based on the books she'd read of her father's—but she couldn't imagine they knew all of it.

She put down her soda. "So, we have been dependent on you for..."

Josh munched on his sandwich, then said, "Vitamin C, sugar,

salt, a few vaccines that we insist you use, and seeds."

"Seeds? I thought that we gathered and used our own seeds."

He finished his sandwich, and balled the wrapper up, and threw it in a container next to his desk. "Some, but unlike on Earth, here, you can't get enough seeds back to continue the crops. Some things in the soil slowly degrade the crops' capacity. We've been working on re-engineering the seeds for Yagan IV, and we give you better and better seeds every year--but you'll still need them from us for the foreseeable future."

Melinda said, "So without this help..."

"You would all be dead."

Melinda was having a hard time taking this all in. Even though she'd hated the life she'd known, it was all she had known, and finding out that it had been *such* a complete sham was difficult for her. What was it all for?

She finished her sandwich and drink in thoughtful silence.

"Alright, Melinda, shall we continue?"

She nodded. She wasn't in as good of a mood as she had been when she arrived.

"This next set of questions requires you to do some manipulation. Just a second."

There was suddenly a ball floating in midair in front of her. She had no idea how it had gotten there.

"Ignore, please, for the moment, the fact that this thing is floating, and you have no idea why. Just touch it and rotate it with your hands."

She reached out and put her fingers on it. There was a very slight resistance to her touch, but when she squeezed harder, her hands went through the ball.

"Don't squeeze too hard."

She eased up and moved the object around.

"Alright. Here are four shapes. That sphere fits into one of these shapes. Find the one that fits. You can rotate these shapes as well."

It was an easy one. The second shape was another ball, but it had a hole the size of the first ball. She moved the first ball and stuck it into the second one.

"Good. Again."

This time, it was a square. She again easily found the shape that it could fit into. This kept going, and the shapes got more and more complex. It was harder and harder to find a fit, but she was able to after moving around the other shapes. She was enjoying herself.

There were more odd tests, but she enjoyed most of them, except for the definition questions that seemed to pop up far too often. She hardly ever knew any of them and felt distressed by them. And there were the odd questions that seemed to be getting at something she couldn't figure out, like her attitudes or reactions to things.

She had just finished a fun set of puzzles that involved arranging symbols to create specific actions when Josh said, "We're done."

"Done?"

"Yes. You've just spent 8 hours with a few brief breaks. Aren't you tired?"

"I guess a little. But it was mostly fun."

"Now, that's an unusual thing for me to hear. What was the least fun?"

"Those definition questions, and the vague questions where I was supposed to say how I felt in reading something."

"Well, that doesn't surprise me. There is a lot you don't know, but you'll learn. "

She nodded.

"Hey, how was it?"

She turned to see Tristan, who had entered the room.

"It was mostly fun."

"Fun, eh? OK, well, I'm glad. I hated it, didn't I, Josh?"

Josh smiled, "She hated every minute, pretty much. The results are just about ready. I have a few things I need to review by hand, but I'll have my system send the results to you later this evening."

"Alright. Copy Drew on it, will you?"

"Right, of course. I can even recommend a teacher for Melinda based on her aptitudes."

"Sounds great. C'mon Melinda, I'm treating you to some ice cream."

"Ice cream?"

Josh said, "You'll love it--I promise."

Melinda got up and followed Tristan out. They stopped at a small storefront, where many people were in line. While waiting, Melinda was quiet, not asking her standard stream of questions, and Tristan wondered what was happening.

She looked at Melinda and said, "What's up, kiddo? You are very quiet this afternoon."

Melinda just shook her head. "Nothing really."

Tristan didn't believe it for a moment, but she let it go. When they got inside the store, Tristan said, "There are a lot of different flavors, but why don't we just try vanilla for now, eh?"

Melinda nodded mutely.

"Two cones, one scoop each, vanilla, please."

She slid her chip over the payment square after the store owner handed her the cones.

"Here you go, Melinda."

Tristan watched as Melinda took a cone and looked around.

She imitated others and licked at the ice cream. Tristan watched her face light up.

Melinda exclaimed, "This is amazing. You can have this any day?"

"Any day, Melinda."

They walked out, ate their cones, and returned to the house. By the time they arrived, Melinda had finished the cone and was licking her fingers.

"That was great!"

"There's a lot like that. You and I grew up in an extremely impoverished setting, Melinda. For a while, everything people here take for granted will seem incredible. But I promise you'll get used to it all."

"But why? What was the point?"

"I wish I could answer that for you. But, if you wish, search for the book 'The Hidden Realm: The Story of the One True Church.' It's the history of the sect that you and I grew up in. It started on Earth, just after First Contact. It was written by someone like us who had grown up with the sect."

Melinda nodded. Tristan could see the cloudy look in her eyes.

"I think I need to rest. It was a long day."

"Do you want House to wake you for dinner? You don't need to--I can leave leftovers for you to eat later."

"I don't think I'll be hungry." Melinda walked upstairs, and Tristan's eyes followed her. Tristan knew that look, the look of despair.

Melinda lay on her bed and couldn't move. She was deeply tired of the unfamiliar, yet the idea of what she had been familiar with felt like anathema to her. She missed her family, especially her sisters and mother, but she never wanted to see them again. She didn't understand half of what most people said in her presence, and when she worked to learn, she discovered vast stores of knowledge about things she'd had no idea even existed.

There was a gentle knock on the door. "Melinda, I don't want to bother you, but..."

"I'm not hungry! Please go away."

"Melinda, it's been two days since you ate something. Please, I care about what happens to you."

"I said, leave me alone!"

She hated Tristan at this moment, although she knew deep inside that there wasn't a good reason for that.

The door opened. "Melinda..."

"What? Please, I'm not hungry."

"Melinda, I think you need to talk with someone. You've not done anything for two weeks, but stay in bed and you haven't eaten anything for days. You need help."

"I don't need help!"

Tristan sat on the bed. "Melinda, you can have a new life now, and you can make up for lost time."

"How can I make up for lost time? I don't know things most five-year-olds know!"

"What do you think about how I've turned out?"

"Well, but you're..."

"I'm what? I'm no different from you, Melinda. In fact, you're smarter than I am, and you knew more than I did when I got here. I didn't even know how to read!"

Melinda sat up. "You didn't?"

"No. It took me a whole year to learn to read."

"Oh. But I can't stand how strange it is here. And I couldn't stand it at home!"

"You've only been here for three weeks, Melinda. Give it some time."

She wasn't convinced at all.

Tristan said, "Look, do me a favor. I have a friend, Dr. Casie Boomer. I think you should talk to her. She's really good at helping people figure things out."

"I don't think she's going to be able to help me!"

"Just humor me, OK?"

Melinda nodded reluctantly.

The next day, she found herself sitting on a couch across from the oldest-looking woman she'd ever seen. Her hair was entirely gray, and her light face had a lot of wrinkles. Even Melinda's grandmother, who had died of old age when Melinda was small, hadn't had so many wrinkles. She seemed very kindly.

"So, Melinda, I'm glad you are here."

Melinda was silent. She didn't have anything to say.

"How are you feeling right now?"

Melinda shifted on the couch. "Fine."

"Really? Is that why you aren't eating?"

"I hate my life!"

Dr. Boomer put her hand on her chin. "Do you hate Tristan?"

"No, no, she's been helpful to me."

"Do you hate your room or the house?"

"No, it's nice."

"OK, so you don't hate Tristan, and you don't hate where you are living now. Do you hate the city?"

"I don't understand the city."

"Is that what you hate? That you don't understand it?"

Melinda threw her hands up. "I hate that my whole life was

a lie, and I didn't learn anything that kids here learn. And I hate my parents and the priest…"

"I understand. You are angry."

"Angry?"

"Yes, you were misled and betrayed, and that makes you angry."

"OK, I guess I'm angry."

"I think it is helpful for you to talk about your life, and we can sort things out."

"It's all a mess."

"I know it feels that way, but trust me, alright?"

Melinda nodded. Melinda spent most of the hour describing her old life to Dr. Boomer, who seemed familiar with it.

"Well, Melinda, I'd like you to come to see me once a week. Would that be alright with you?"

Melinda felt better after talking with her.

"OK, if Tristan is alright with it."

"Yes, she's fine with it, Melinda. I'll see you next week."

Melinda rose and left the room, and walked outside, where Tristan was waiting.

"How was it?"

"It was OK. She wants me to come back next week."

"And is that what you want?" Melinda nodded.

CHAPTER SIX

Kerry was sitting in the captain's chair, thinking about the last few months since the disaster at Rigel. There hadn't been any other hint of invasion, and for the most part, life in space had returned to close to normal, although she could still feel the edge of fear when she talked to other captains. She could still feel it, too, but she did her best to ignore it.

She was brought out of her reverie when Abdul said, "Captain, the traffic up ahead is crazy. We've got to wait five hours to get through the gate. The Olympics are at Diallo II this month."

Kerry swore. She'd forgotten all about the Olympics and had chosen to take the "shorter route" through Diallo, which would have been four jumps to Yagan rather than six jumps. Oh, well, it wasn't the short cut, she thought.

"Alright, well, we're in no real hurry since we don't have any passengers or cargo."

Ainsley said, "Well, I'm in a hurry."

"Oh?" Kerry turned toward Ainsley.

"I'm going to visit Kerwin on McKinney Station Two. It will eat into my shore leave since I have to go back through Diallo again."

Kerry felt her brows rise. "Kerwin?"

"I met him a few months ago while we were at EpYi. He was

on his way to a new posting at McKinney Two. He's very sexy. And smart, too."

"I can't keep track of your men, Ainsley. Anyway, why don't we drop you off at Diallo? I don't think Meadow would mind filling in for you for the two jumps from Diallo to Yagan."

"She just got off duty, Captain! I hate to ask her to do that."

"I don't think she'd mind a whit. Let me ask her... and, yes, I'll ask her politely!"

She pushed the comm button to contact Meadow, who she knew wasn't asleep.

"Hey Meadow, I want to drop Ainsely off at Diallo since she needs to go there anyway to get to McKinney for her shore leave. Do you mind filling in for the last two jumps to Yagan?"

A light voice came out of the comm. "Don't mind at all, Captain, actually happy to. It will keep me busy."

Kerry said, "See?"

Ainsely nodded.

"Why don't you take shuttle three? Jeff just finished the refit, and it needs a good test run of jump capability."

"Thanks, Captain."

"Well, I've now solved my share of problems for the day. I'm going back to my quarters. Let me know if you need me."

She left the control room and headed down to her quarters. It had been a solid eight months since they'd had shore leave and three months since she'd been to Yagan. The last visit to Tristan had been sweet but way too short. This time, she was going to get to stay for two weeks.

She thought back to the first time she'd met Tristan. Tristan had just finished her education on Yagan, and she was doing some traveling around different systems. Kerry was crew on another ship then, and they had shore leave on McKinney Prime, a delightful little planet that was very pastoral and peaceful. She had some old friends on McKinney, and she was at a party that Tristan had also been invited to.

She smiled when she remembered the Tristan of those days. Naive as all get out, vulnerable, and irresistibly cute. Tristan was still irresistibly cute to Kerry, but she wasn't naive or vulnerable anymore. She very much missed Tristan. Her thoughts wandered elsewhere, spurred by worry.

Not much more had been learned about what happened on Rigel. The eyewitness accounts, including theirs, and any automated surveillance systems had painted a picture of a completely unknown species that, for reasons that were still mysterious, at least to the public, destroyed everything human in the system and the jumpgate. She remembered that Dr. Greenwald had known it was coming, and she was very curious as to how he knew, but she figured she'd never learn. Although transparency was treasured in the Terran galaxy, some aspects of the workings of Galactic Central had never been opened up. She wasn't quite sure what she thought of that.

She occupied herself with the minutia of business she'd be putting on ice for two weeks. She'd lined up a shipment of live aerawyn, the large, bulky animals initially imported to Yagan IV from another far-flung colony but had become numerous there. They were apparently related to oxen from Earth but had been modified to work in dryer, hotter climates. Kerry had only seen them once; they were almost twice as large as most oxen and had very light white hairs all over their bodies. Apparently, some other colony on Jenkins II, which had a very similar climate and biosphere to Yagan IV, wanted to see if they could raise them. Jenkins wasn't the greatest place to get cargo, but several passengers wanted transport, so she'd take them on.

"Captain?" Abdul's voice spoke from the comm.

"What's up?"

"Just wanted to let you know that Ainsley is off, and we're next in line for the jump to Burness. According to traffic reports, we should be in the Yagan system in three hours."

"Thanks, Abdul."

They got to the Yagan system and entered orbit around Yagan IV.

Jeff was the only crew member who had chosen to stay aboard for this shore leave. The fact that he almost never went on shore leaves worried Kerry until she realized that he really did enjoy being on the ship alone, working, more than anything else. For him, a vacation meant the joy of two weeks without any other crew in his hair or destinations to arrive at so he could take apart what needed to be taken apart. Some of the rest of the crew took shuttle two to Wezlar; one jump out from Yagan, and a much more cosmopolitan place to spend shore leave.

After she and a few crew landed the shuttle on Yagan, she walked the familiar streets to Tristan's house, and stood in front of the door. A young woman with kinky, dark hair tied back, answered the door.

"Hi, you must be Kerry! Tristan was expecting you. She went to the market to get some vegetables for dinner. She said to tell you to make yourself at home. I'm Melinda."

She stuck out her hand, and Kerry shook it. They walked into the living room, and Kerry dropped her bag.

"Can I get you something to drink? Tristan said your usual was here. Of course, I don't know what that is..."

"It'll be a cylinder marked 'Yagan SoBrew.'"

"Oh, the beer. Sure, I'll get you some."

"Have you tried it?"

Melinda laughed. "I'm not allowed yet. Tristan is strict about some things."

Ah, yes. Kerry was reminded of that particular trait of Tristan—following the rules—a holdover from her days growing up as she did. She wondered if Melinda would have that trait or not.

Melinda handed Kerry the cold beer, and Kerry sank gratefully into the couch's cushions. She was more tired than she realized. It had been a stressful time since Rigel. She regarded Melinda, who seemed a little bit nervous.

"How long have you been here?"

"Three months."

"Long enough to be used to some things, but not long enough to understand much."

The girl nodded.

"I had a rough couple of months. Things are smoothing out now. It helps that I'm enjoying most of what I'm learning, and I can find my way around most places now."

"What are you studying?"

"About half of my studies are basic—I have to catch up."

Kerry sensed some resentment in her voice.

"The other half is mostly math and programming, with some science."

"Ah, so you have the aptitude for those?"

"Yes. I have some aptitude for language. A little for music, not much for art. A lot for math and programming."

"That's fun stuff."

"It is. I'm enjoying it. It's fun to learn how to manipulate things, whether they are real or not."

Kerry smiled and wondered idly whether Melinda would end up becoming a spacer.

The door opened, and Tristan arrived, holding bags of groceries. Kerry smiled. As usual, when Kerry visited, Tristan went all out to get good food for them.

"Hey, let me help you with that."

Kerry got up went to Tristan, and took a couple of the bags. They looked into each other's eyes and kissed briefly. She was so happy to be back—it felt a lot like coming home.

"I take it you two have made your acquaintances."

Kerry said, "We have, indeed. She got me a beer."

"Well, I've got a great welcome back dinner planned for you, love—stuff you really enjoy. The tomatoes are heavenly now, and I even got a few avocados. Melinda, I don't think you've had the pleasure of those, have you?"

"Nope, not yet."

The three of them put the groceries away, and Tristan started to prepare the meal.

"Melinda, do you mind chopping the onions and garlic?"

"Nope."

"Kerry, love, go sit in the living room and relax. We'll handle this."

She went back to the living room quite happily. She was tired, and it was nice just sipping her beer and watching the two women prepare dinner. Melinda had learned her way around the kitchen.

Tristan said, "House, play some twencen jazz, please, heavy on the Coltrane. Medium volume."

Kerry relaxed as the strains of "Soul Eyes" and "'Round Midnight" came through the room. It was good to be here.

"What music is that?" It was Melinda's question.

Kerry said, "It's a type of music called jazz.' It's mostly from the twentieth century on Earth, although there are still some musicians who make original jazz now. I love jazz so much that I named my ship after one of its luminaries, John Coltrane."

"I've never heard music like that. The only music I'd ever heard before I got here was hymns in church. We weren't allowed any other music. Tristan has introduced me to 'Classic Rock and Roll.'"

Kerry laughed. "Tristan is a fan of it. We both love twentieth-century music. For me, it's because it's uncomplicated, and for Tristan, it's because it's freeing. Right?" She could see Tristan nodding.

"I played The Clash for her first."

"The Clash? First? Tristan!"

"Well, I figured anything after that would seem tame."

Kerry commented, "I guess that's true. Anyway, music after First Contact is just... too complicated for me."

Melinda said, "I've been reading about First Contact. It seems like it was a really unsettling event for humans."

Kerry said, "It was. Think about it: we didn't have any evidence that we weren't alone, and we had hundreds or thousands of years of thinking that Earth was the only planet that God made, you know. And science had shown that it was likely that other planets had life, but none of them were speaking to us. Then, one day, a ship starts building a jumpgate. And they say something cryptic like 'It's time.'"

Tristan said, "Well, we were about to do ourselves in. I think that's what they meant."

Kerry answered, "Yeah, we were."

Melinda said, "I'm intrigued by the jumpgate tenders. They keep themselves far from other species, yet they make and tend the jumpgates, which seems like such a gift."

Kerry said, "Most galactic species have adopted the attitude of the Korth, who are considered our benefactors--the ones who came through the newly-build jumpgate first, to help us out, and help us get our bearings. The Korth feel that each species of the galaxy has one gift to give all of the others. For them, it's introducing new species to the galaxy, for the jumpgate tenders, it's the jumpgates, for the Zohalo, it's the agricultural technology that all species that eat plant matter have benefited from."

"What is our gift?"

"I don't think we've figured it out yet, Melinda. And that bothers a lot of people."

"Do the Korth know?"

"If they do, they aren't telling."

Tristan said, "OK, enough philosophy. Dinner is ready!"

They had a very pleasant dinner, and then Melinda left to go to her room, and Kerry had Tristan all to herself. They playfully cleaned up dinner and then sat together on the couch.

Tristan said, "So, love, how are you? I heard about Rigel and the aftermath. I was so glad you got out in time! And the whole climate now sounds stressful."

"Yes, we were so lucky! I likely wouldn't be here now if it hadn't been for a broken engineering system."

"I don't even want to think about that, love!"

"I know, I know! Being at EpYi was chaotic, and getting all those passengers to where they wanted to go took a lot longer than I thought it would. People are really nervous about this whole thing. They feel like they have no idea what system is next. Galactic Central is trying to make us feel better, and they clearly know something they are not sharing... yet. But it set my whole schedule on its ear and, at the same time, is shifting people's priorities. Commerce is just not the same anymore."

"Do you think it will settle down?"

"I do. I've already got a full docket of cargo and passengers for the next two months, so I think it will be fine. It's a good thing I'm a well-regarded captain. I think it's been tough for some of the newer or less well-known ships."

Tristan touched Kerry's forehead. "How are you doing, love? How's Melinda?"

"It's been rough. It's smoothing out now, but she was devastated for a while there."

"More than you?"

"Way more than me. She wouldn't eat for a week, leave her room, or do anything. I tried to talk to her. I finally got her to see Dr. Boomer, and she is slowly moving her way out of it, but I don't think she's out of the woods yet."

"Why do you think she's had such a hard time?"

"I didn't much like my life when I was there, and when I found out I could just be banished, I did what I could to accomplish that. She absolutely hated her life and was determined to run away, but somehow, when she was faced with the fact that the life she hated so much was a sham that some guy had invented a couple of hundred years before, she just lost it. I think she was angrier than she knew what to do with, so she turned it inside."

"I can't even imagine how hard that could be."

"For a week, she couldn't stop talking about how she would go back and tell everyone what a sham it was, and I kept having to tell her she couldn't ever go back. She'd get thrown in prison if she tried."

"It's hard for me to accept that they have the right to do what they want. People grow up there and have no idea that they can live a full, complete life."

"Yeah, you and a lot of people. There have been several attempts at Galactic Congress to outlaw colonies like that, or at least force the children to be educated about their choices. I don't doubt that someday, one of those attempts will succeed. It's one of the reasons I think I stuck around--I would have liked to have gotten to be someone who enforces that law when it comes around."

"Past tense, Tristan?"

"I'm done, Kerry. I'm getting too old for this."

"Tristan, you are barely thirty!"

"Melinda has made me realize I've done my duty here. After I finish raising her, I'm leaving. Time for me to move on."

"Well, you always know you have a place on the *John Coltrane* if you want it. But you might not want it."

Tristan smiled. "I would love to be with you, Kerry, but my presence on the ship introduces complications... besides, I'm not sure I'm meant for space. I'm a lawyer, you know."

Kerry said, "Hey, I don't really want to talk anymore..."

The next morning, as she was lying in bed, Kerry looked next to her at her lover, who was still sleeping, her arm flopped over her head. She loved Tristan more than she'd loved anyone in her life, and although she wanted more than anything to be with Tristan all the time, she respected Tristan's need to define her own life. The *John Coltrane* defined Kerry's and would until she tired of it, and was ready to stop working, and settle somewhere peaceful.

Tristan stirred and opened her eyes.

"Morning, sunshine." Tristan smiled.

"Morning. Have any idea what you want to do today?"

"Nothing. That is, I want to do nothing."

Tristan smiled. That was the way it always was for Kerry the first few days back. She needed to do nothing for a while. It was fine; Tristan had enough on her plate anyway.

"Alright. Make yourself at home, of course. I need to take

Melinda in for a check-up and then introduce her to her programming teacher."

"Already?"

"She's amazing at it. I mean really amazing. She's been learning it for a month and a half, and I've been told she's already writing good, usable code. She's a natural. Kolwin Porter is going to be her teacher."

"Kolwin Porter? He lives here?"

"No, no, he lives back on Earth. A copy of Kolwin Porter's artificial teaching system is going to be her teacher. Josh put in a request right after he found out what her programming aptitude was. It's pretty tough to get a copy of his teaching system. Lots of competition for it."

"It's not like he couldn't make infinite copies."

"He doesn't like to. He only has ten."

"And Melinda has one?"

"Yup."

"Wow."

"Yeah, amazing, eh? I think we have a prodigy."

"Well, if she really is, I bet she'll get sucked up by Epsilon Eridani."

"I don't know. She doesn't seem the type, does she?"

"True. A little too well-rounded, perhaps."

"We'll see. She'll do this and can decide when she's done with her education."

They got up, dressed, and wandered downstairs, where Melinda had already cooked a nice breakfast.

Tristan said, "Melinda! Thanks, girl."

"I figured you wanted to sleep in, and I hadn't cooked breakfast in a while."

They sat down to eat, and Kerry said, "I hear you'll be learning coding from the best."

"Yes, I'm excited. The teaching system just got loaded into our home system yesterday."

"You like coding?"

"I love it. I'm jealous of the other students I've met who've been studying it for ten years. I have so much to catch up with."

Tristan said, "Don't worry about it--you will."

"I know, but I still resent the whole thing."

Kerry's two weeks went by quickly, and before she knew it, she was standing next to Tristan in the shuttle launch area.

"I'll see you in about three months. I've got an order from your Ag department for a shipment from the Zohalo that they left on McKinney Station three. I can stay a couple of nights."

"I look forward to it. I miss you already, Kerry. Have a good trip."

"Hey, I can tell you are taking good care of Melinda. She appreciates you, even if she doesn't say it."

"I know."

"Bye."

"Bye."

They kissed, and Kerry entered the shuttle, where her crew awaited her.

"Alright, y'all, let's get this bucket back to the *John Coltrane.*"

As they arrived in the shuttle launch zone on the *John Coltrane,* Kerry could see that both other shuttles were back. That was good; she wouldn't have to spend time hunting the crew down. Kerry returned to the control room and started the pre-launch checks. Ainsley was there.

Kerry asked, "So, how was the boy?"

"Not as great as I thought."

"Sorry about that."

"It was still fun, but he's a bit traditional."

"Traditional?"

"Yeah, he wanted to talk about a *relationship* before we slept together."

"So?"

"So, I had to wait like five days of my shore leave before we had sex. It was frustrating."

Sex-crazed was not a word she would generally use to describe Ainsley, but sometimes...

"Sorry about that. So, strike him off the list?"

"Sadly, yeah. When we left, he asked me to marry him, and stay on McKinney. I told him he was nuts. I'm a spacer and will always be a spacer. And besides, I said, I'm not the marrying type."

"And?"

"He was pretty upset."

"I see. Not another ex to visit, eh?"

"Nope. In a year, he'll find someone and settle down, you know. It won't be me. How's my girl Tristan?"

"She's fine. We had a good time."

"Who's she fostering now?"

"A sweet kid named Melinda. Apparently, a coding prodigy. She's getting to use one of Kolwin Porter's teaching systems to learn from."

Gaylin said, "No, really? You're kidding! Do you know how hard those are to get? Thousands of kids on Epsilon Eridani want one, and some kid on Yagan IV got one? Wow."

"Yeah. All the more astonishing since she was in this cult colony and didn't even know that programming existed three months ago!"

Gaylin whistled, and Kerry wondered if it were with some envy. Gaylin always felt a little inferior to the coders on Epsilon, but Kerry knew he probably could do much better. Those kids were too narrowly focused and isolated to make the necessary leaps to do useful work. Perhaps that was something Kolwin Porter knew.

"OK, are we ready?"

Gaylin said, "All systems are up and ready."

She touched her comm and said, "Jeff, status?"

"Everything's happy, cap'n. The ship and I had a very nice vacation. I tore apart the port engine manifold, the stern ion stream, and several sensor systems and put them back nice and ready for our next trip."

"Alright. Ainsley?"

"Course to the Yagan jumpgate plotted, as is the course to the Wayfar gate to Jenkins."

She pushed the comm again. "Sevy, how are our charges?"

"Sedated, so they are quiet. I do hope we get to Jenkins in time. The sedation should wear off in about five hours."

"Thanks for that info."

"Abdul, tell the jumpgate system we're a go."

A pause. "First in line, Captain."

Kerry said, "When does that ever happen?"

Ainsley said, "When were at Yagan, almost every time. It's a backwater, cap'n."

"Yes, but it's my backwater. Let's go, shall we?"

CHAPTER SEVEN

House said, "Melinda, Tristan says that dinner is ready."

Melinda had just finished a session with Dr. Porter. It was funny to call the system by the author's name, but it seemed so real. His holographic image would sit near her as she worked at her desk and comment on what she was doing at varied intervals.

She was building a complex system to manage a hydroponics garden. A month ago, she had spent a week in the gardens, learning about how it worked, and Dr. Porter always gave her assignments that were connected to her real-world explorations.

"Goodbye, Dr. Porter. It's time for dinner."

"Alright, Melinda. I'll see you tomorrow." His image faded.

Once downstairs she saw Tristan putting food on the table and asked, "Can I help?"

"Nope, it's all done. You can clean up."

"OK."

They sat down to eat.

Tristan asked, "So, how was your day? Mostly programming?"

"Yeah. I'm writing an improved hydroponics control system."

"Oh?"

"Yeah, if it passes all the tests, it might even replace the one we have now. And I've had to learn a ton of biology and chemistry in the process. It's really fun."

Tristan said, "Well, better you than me."

"You don't like that stuff?"

"I'm a people person, Melinda. I do well working with people to get things done. I manage, coordinate, etc. But I'm not like you. For instance, I spent most of the afternoon with the Port Committee."

"What does the Port Committee do?"

"The Port Committee negotiates with the Space Guild, which represents captains, about issues regarding trade and the like."

"What do you do on the committee?"

"I'm the chair of the negotiations subcommittee, so I do the negotiations with the Guild, mostly around berthing and custom fees."

"Fees?"

"Yes, when each captain arrives at Yagan IV, they pay a small berthing fee, and a customs fee if they are bringing any items to Yagan IV. It pays for the upkeep of the port, and for the inspection of items, etc."

"Oh, that makes sense."

"But of course, the Guild wants those fees to be as low as possible, and we want them to be as high as possible. So, we need to talk each year and come to an amicable arrangement."

"So, you spent the afternoon talking about the fees with the Guild?"

"No, I spent the afternoon reporting on my conversations to the full committee."

"Why didn't you just write a report, like the reports I've read from the hydroponics management group?"

"I did. But I have to explain it and answer questions."

"That would frustrate me!"

"I know. See what I mean?"

Melinda nodded.

After Melinda cleaned up dinner, Tristan said, "Melinda, I want to show you something."

"Alright."

"Sit." She sat on one of the couches in the living room.

"House, play Star Trek, Original series, um, let's see, the episode with the Tribbles."

The screen grew in mid-air, and some music started playing.

A voice said, "This is the voyage of the starship Enterprise. Her five-year mission is to boldly go where no man has gone before."

It was a little mystifying to Melinda. It looked to be an old Earth movie of some sort--she'd heard Tristan and others mention these, but she'd never seen one. She'd seen her first sim a few weeks ago, where the living room became a forest, and she got to see and take part in an adventure herself. This was different--it was two-dimensional, and she could tell she could have no influence on how things turned out.

When it was over, Tristan said, "That was an old Earth television show, one of the first popular shows that depicted interstellar travel. Of course, we still think that nothing can travel faster than light, so they probably did get that part wrong. But it is fun to see what people were imagining before First Contact. It was very popular, leading to ten other series and over fifty movies. There are a few sims, as well."

"Do people explore the galaxy like they imagined?"

"Not really. The jumpgate tenders do--they are very long-lived, and they send out ships to very far-flung places so that they can construct new gates. We can't do that, so we depend on them. But we have settled more than a hundred systems in the galaxy, and there are probably another fifty human-habitable planets out there with gates."

"Wow, that's a lot. Are there people who go to those new planets and start colonies?"

"Yes, there are."

"Is Kerry one?"

"No. Kerry is one of the spacers that ferries people and stuff between established colonies. She likes that kind of work; she's not much of an explorer."

"I'd love to explore."

"Yes, I get that impression from you. If that's what you want to do, you can do that. The corps at Epsilon Eridani might be sad, though."

"I don't want just to do programming my whole life. I mean, I love it, but I want to see stuff- see this galaxy. I'm just now learning that it exists."

"Well, it will be time for you to choose an apprenticeship in a year. You might ask Kerry--she does take on apprentices on occasion."

"Really? That would be fun--I'd get to see a lot."

"That you would."

"OK, I'll ask her next time she's here."

A couple of weeks later, Tristan told Melinda that they would have a guest for dinner. She was being mysterious about it, and Melinda wondered who it was. She'd met most of Tristan's friends, a few of whom were from the colony. She'd also met a lot of people her age and had begun to strike up a couple of friendships. One in particular felt very satisfying--it was with Shawnita Loch, who had grown up in the village next to hers. She hadn't known Shawnita, or Nita as she wanted to be called, but the two villages did a lot of things together, and it was familiar to Maxlinda. It was nice to have a friend who had some of the same experiences and knew some of the same people.

She had spent the day studying climate science, which was something she enjoyed. She still had no idea what she wanted to do with her life, but she did know she wanted to apprentice on a spaceship and hoped that Kerry would be willing to host her.

She walked down the stairs and could smell the aerawyn roast cooking.

"Mm mm, I like the way you make aerawyn roast. It's so much better than my mother's, and my mother was considered one of the best aerawyn cooks in our village."

"Well, I have the benefit of a lot of herbs and spices your mother doesn't."

"I guess that's true. So, who's the guest?"

"His name is Luke. He's also one of the banished, and he lived here for a couple of years. He was banished from your village five years ago."

"Luke Vargas?"

"Yes! You knew him?"

"Sort of. He was the older brother of a friend of mine. He was a nice guy. My friend was really upset when he disappeared, and no adults would tell her where he went."

"Well, now you know what happened to him."

"Do you know why he was banished?"

"I'll let him explain it to you."

"So, what's for dinner besides aerawyn?"

"We've got some tato fries, and salad. Ice cream for dessert."

"Sounds yummy."

House said, "Tristan, Luke is at the door."

Tristan put down the towel she had in her hand and walked to the door. She opened it, and Melinda recognized Luke immediately, although he didn't seem to have the ready smile that she remembered.

"Hey, Luke, come in!" They hugged. "I'd like to re-introduce you to Melinda St. John."

He walked in. When he looked at her, he smiled. "I remember you. Janice's friend."

"Yeah." They hugged.

"How is she?"

"She was fine last I saw her. Married."

"To?"

"Maurice Williams."

"No, really? Sucky. I'm glad I didn't see that."

Melinda laughed. Maurice had bullied Melinda and her younger sister horribly and wasn't someone most people liked.

"Luke, dinner is just about ready. Why don't you help Melinda set the table?"

Luke knew his way around the kitchen and dining room, and in no time, they'd set the table. Tristan got all of the food to the table, and they sat down to eat.

Tristan said, "Luke, I'm glad to see you. It's been too long."

"I'm sorry that I've been uncommunicative. I wanted to wait to tell you the good news."

"Oh?"

"I decided to train as a medic. I was accepted into the program and started classes last month. I love it."

"Oh, Luke, I'm so glad to hear it! Why didn't you want to tell me?"

"I was afraid they wouldn't take me, and I didn't want you to know if they didn't."

"Luke..."

"It's OK, really. Anyway, they took me, and it's great."

Melinda asked, "How long is the training?"

"Three years of classes and such, then two years of apprenticeship."

Tristan asked, "Do you want to stay here, or leave?"

"I want to stay here. This is my home. I'm thinking of starting a medic outreach program when I'm finished with my training."

Melinda asked, "Medic outreach?"

"I want to offer training and help to the colonist doctors, who have very few resources."

Tristan said, "Ambitious, and..."

Luke said, "Unrealistic. But I want to try anyway. So, Melinda, what are you studying?"

"Mostly math, programming and science. I love it all. I want to apprentice on a spaceship."

Luke smiled. "That sounds perfect for you. I remember Janice used to tell me things that you'd told her from the books you stole from your father."

"She did?"

"Yup."

Melinda said, "Tristan, Janice is the one that I got caught with."

Luke said, "Caught with?"

"We were lying in a barn snuggling without our shirts on. It happened after you left."

"I see. One of your sins, I take it?"

"Yeah. The one that got me banished was exploring."

"They finally caught you at it?"

"Yeah, I got injured doing it one day, and had to be carried back to town. I was banished right then."

"I'm sorry about that."

"I'm not, Luke. I'm glad I'm gone. Why did you get banished?"

"I got the priest's wife pregnant."

"Britta is your child?"

"Yup. Shelly and I were in love. She was forced to marry the priest so young, after his first wife died, and she hated him. We were trying to figure out how to get him to divorce her, so we could marry."

"How did they find out?"

"Well, neither Shelly nor I knew that the priest was infertile. When she got pregnant, she told him as if it was his. When he explained that it couldn't be, and she'd better tell him who the father was, she caved. Next thing I knew I was here."

"Well, the priest is raising Britta as his own. No one knows that she's not. But now I know why Shelly is so unhappy. I guess I figured it was just because she had to be with him. I'm sorry, Luke. So, you would have stayed if you could?"

"Yes. But Melinda, I've learned so much, and I know now that no one should be forced to live that way. I just wish we could do something about it."

Tristan said, "The last colony autonomy bill passed Galactic Council without the rider about imposing education on the youth of insular colonies. One day, I hope it does."

After Luke left, and Melinda was putting the dishes away, she said to Tristan, "Thanks for having him over. It was nice to see him and hear his story."

"I figured you'd appreciate it. It took him a long time to find his way. I'm glad he has, now."

A week later, Melinda was walking through a part of the city. Luke had invited her to hang out and have dinner with some of his friends at his apartment. Melinda knew that Nita would be there as well. She was looking forward to seeing Luke again and meeting more kids who had been banished from the colony.

She was feeling much more at ease with her life. Things were no longer so unfamiliar, although once in a while, she still was taken aback by something. Ice cream still seemed so miraculous to her--the colony had no electricity and no refrigeration, so they never had anything frozen. And sugar was so carefully rationed, that she rarely had had anything sweet. The combination of those two, and the creaminess, still surprised her when she had it.

She walked down the street that had Luke's building and found 75 Athol Lane. She entered the building, which had an atrium, and walked up to the second floor. Luke's apartment was number 2G. She stood in front of the door, and it was opened by a stocky woman with long blond hair that she'd never met.

"Hi, I'm Melinda."

"Hey, Melinda, I'm Joan. C'mon in."

There were about ten people scattered about on chairs and couches. She waved to Nita, who was the only one she knew. Luke came out of the kitchen.

"Hey, Melinda! Everyone, this here is Melinda. She came from Revelation."

Melinda sat down, and everyone introduced themselves, and what village they were from. In conversation, some of them knew people in common. Amos and Chalcedon were relatively close to Revelation, and often people married between villages.

Luke had cooked up a great meal, very traditional. Aerawyn roast, tato mash, maso cactus, and beans. Melinda guiltily had her first beer. She definitely enjoyed the mellow, warm feeling it gave her.

After a while, the kids filtered out, and she was left with Joan and Luke, cleaning up.

Melinda said, "Thanks, Luke! That was a wonderful dinner."

"I enjoyed making it. I like cooking our food. I miss it sometimes."

Joan said, "It was nice to have it, but I have to admit I don't miss it so much. I've gotten pretty used to things like tomatoes and greens."

"Yeah, me too," said Melinda. "So Joan, what are you studying?"

"I'm studying inter-species relations. I'd like to be a Galactic Foreign Service agent."

"Like get stationed on an alien planet?"

"Yup!"

"I hear that's hard work. You might end up somewhere where you have to stay inside most of the time."

"Sure, you have to do that sort of thing for a while. But if you do well, and move up the ladder, you get posted somewhere like Irridis Prime."

"Irridis Prime?"

"Yeah. It's like forty jumps from the closest Terran colony, so it's really far away, but I've heard it's one of the most amazing planets. It has a breathtaking atmosphere and is an amazingly verdant, gorgeous planet, and the aliens there are very peaceful and spiritual."

"That sounds really cool. Maybe someday I'll visit you there. I want to be a spacer and explore the galaxy."

"That sounds like fun."

Luke said, "And I'll be happy staying here, exploring the galaxy of the human body."

Joan stroked Luke's arm. "He really loves studying to be a medic. It's too bad I can't convince him to leave with me when I'm done with my studies. He could get a posting anywhere."

"But I want to stay here, sweetheart. Yagan IV is my home. And someday, the colony will open up. I know it will."

"You are being unrealistic, but I love you anyway."

Melinda watched them for a moment, feeling some envy. She did wish that at some point, she could find someone. She knew it would happen.

"Thanks, again, Luke. I'm going to head home."

"Thanks for helping us clean up, Melinda."

"Sure thing. See you later."

CHAPTER EIGHT

Kerry and Dr. Greenwald exited the shuttle and walked through the dusty ground of the Yagan IV shuttle landing area. She could see Tristan and Melinda standing near the entrance. They walked toward them, and she and Tristan embraced.

"Hey, thanks for the nice greeting. And hi, Melinda!"

"Hi, Kerry."

"Abdul, this is Tristan and Melinda. And Tristan and Melinda, this is one of our passengers, Dr. Greenwald. He has a short official stop here."

As she looked at Dr. Greenwald, she realized he was staring at Melinda—more specifically, at her chest. She hadn't ever seen this behavior from him, and she was mystified.

"Excuse me," Dr. Greenwald said to Melinda.

"Yes?"

"Where did you get that pendant?" He said it with a kind of intensity that Kerry hadn't heard from him before. She now, at least, understood this behavior better.

"Well..."

"*Where* did you get it?" It was almost shouted. Tristan moved to protect Melinda.

"She brought it with her. She's from the colony here."

"So, the pendant is from *here?*"

Melinda nodded. "I found it."

"Where?"

"Why do you want to know?"

"I can't explain it now, but I want you to understand that it is of the utmost importance that you explain exactly where you got that pendant. And I mean *exactly.*"

Melinda looked petrified, and Kerry wasn't sure it was just Dr. Greenwald's manner.

Tristan quietly said to Melinda, "It's OK. You can tell him. Nothing bad will happen to you."

"Well, the day I was banished, I had been exploring. I mean, that was why I was banished. Anyway, there is this cave that I liked to go to a lot. And I was exploring a part of it I'd never been. At one point, I found a kind of plate in the cave floor, and I tried to open it up, but the cave floor collapsed, and I found myself in this room, with all of these strange things. I looked around for a while, but then I was afraid I would be late getting back. So, I gathered up a few small items, just for fun, then climbed out. As I was climbing out, the whole cave collapsed, and I was pushed out by the collapse."

Tristan said, "She was very badly injured."

"You have other items?"

"Some of these circles, a couple of cylindrical things, and a few other things."

"I really need to see them."

Kerry said, "What is this about, Dr. Greenwald?"

"This is about Rigel. That much, I will say now. Can you have Melinda bring those other things to the Yagan diplomatic office? That's where I have my meeting."

Tristan said, "Yes, we can do that."

He said, "Thank you, thank you very much. You may be saving many lives today." And then he walked off quickly.

Tristan said, "You OK, Melinda?"

"Sure, I just don't understand."

Kerry said, "Neither do we, yet. Let's go get that stuff and go meet him, shall we?"

They all walked toward Tristan's place in silence. Melinda went up to her room and gathered all of the artifacts. There were more than she remembered, and she guessed that was a good thing. She walked back down and handed them all to Kerry in a small bag. She also took off her pendant and gave it to her.

Kerry handed it back. "No keep it unless we have to give it to him."

She nodded. They walked to the diplomatic office and asked at the front desk for Dr. Greenwald. They were ushered into a conference room that was currently full of people. Kerry looked at Melinda, who looked stunned and scared. She could understand. The room was hushed, with serious faces all around.

Kerry took the bag with the artifacts and gave it to Dr. Greenwald.

"Please, have a seat. You should also hear this."

He spread out the artifacts and took a deep breath. Kerry could tell he was very disturbed.

The Chair said loudly, "Please, may we have your attention! Thank you. I wish to introduce Dr. Horace Greenwald from Galactic Central, Alien Threat office."

"Thank you. I came to Yagan IV to give my report to this interstellar committee about the situation surrounding Rigel. Galactic Central has decided that it was time to begin to spread the information more widely, with public disclosure following. However, little did I know how important this visit would become.

"Let me show you all something." He pushed some icons on a tablet, and four images popped over the conference table.

"The first image is the live picture of one of the cylindrical artifacts that Melinda St. John found in a cave here, on Yagan IV. The second is an artifact found in a cave on Rigel III. The third is an artifact found in a cave on Segaris II, and the fourth is an artifact found on Zetalu VI. As you can see, they all are identical."

There were some murmurs in the room. Kerry had never heard of either Segaris II or Zetalu VI. They must be uninhabited.

"Eighteen years ago, I was on a dig on Zetalu VI, a backwater planet with no intelligent species and no material interest to Terrans. There had been a spectacular find of old artifacts, perhaps millions of years old, and I was there with a small expedition, doing my doctoral dissertation. While we were digging, the planet was attacked. I barely managed to get away with my life in the shuttle. The ship that brought us had been destroyed, as was the jumpgate. It took us three years to make it to the nearest jumpgate, and we would have starved, except we happened to come across a Terran derelict with intact food supplies."

"Segaris II was attacked ten years ago, and the jumpgate was destroyed. I'd been there several years earlier because a relic hunter had found some interesting artifacts that matched the ones I found earlier at Zetalu VI. One month before Rigel was invaded, I had come across a scientific paper showing these artifacts were found on Rigel. I was on my way to Rigel to warn them and investigate further.

"There are four other planets where these artifacts have been found, but none of them were inhabited. Over the last ten years, it has been determined that each has now had their jump gates destroyed.

"Thus, the conclusion is that Yagan is most likely next. We must evacuate the entire Yagan system as soon as possible. We have no idea when they are coming, but they will destroy everything. That is what they do."

Someone in the room asked, "Why? Can't we talk with them?"

"I asked our benefactors, the Korth, whether they know about this species, but they do not. The artifacts have been dated to least a million years old--much older than any species we are in contact with. No one knows about this species. The current theory is that they left the galaxy, or perhaps went to a small corner of it far away, but have returned for some unknown reason.

"But that's just a theory. What we know for certain is that every one of the eight systems where these artifacts have been found has been attacked and jump gates destroyed before anyone could do anything or even try to communicate with them. The danger is too high to risk not evacuating Yagan. I have sent a request to Galactic Central for aid in this effort. I expect that we'll get help within two days. We need to prepare the colonists."

Tristan said, "Sir, you have no idea what you are saying. We can evacuate Yagan City – that's the easy part. There is only one colony on this planet, about 40,000 colonists. But they will refuse to leave. I can almost guarantee it."

"They would rather die than leave?"

"Let's just say that they will choose to trust God rather than people from the 'wilderness of the unbelievers.'"

"What?"

"I grew up among them."

"Galactic Central will order them to leave."

"That may be, but I can tell you it's going to be a nightmare to get them to leave."

"We have no choice."

Kerry was stunned. The whole thing felt unimaginable. She got up, left the room, and opened the pocket communication to the ship.

"Ainsley."

"Yes, captain?"

"We're staying here for a while. Believe it or not, there is a big emergency, and they must evacuate Yagan IV."

"Evacuate? What?"

"I'll explain later. We'll need to prepare the crew and ship for many passengers."

"Evacuating a whole planet?"

"Luckily, there's only about seventy thousand here, so it won't be that big a deal."

"But still…"

"Yeah. I know."

"OK, I'll let everyone know."

"I'll be back up in a few hours."

She walked back into an argument. A man she didn't know was shouting.

"We need more evidence than these trinkets found by a *little girl*!"

Tristan said, "Jorge, really. You are being ridiculous. It doesn't matter who found them. These artifacts are on this planet. And every other planet we know about has been destroyed by these aliens. Do you want to risk sticking around? I certainly don't!"

Pandemonium erupted, and finally, Kerry heard the sound of a fist pounding on the table. Eventually, people quieted down.

The Chair said, "It seems we are in danger and must act. I will await the official word of Galactic Central, but in the meanwhile, we should at least begin preparations. I am adjourning this meeting with the request that no one here say anything to anyone, even your families until we get official word from Galactic Central. When that happens, Colony Manager Wilson will then disseminate the evacuation information as she sees fit. Meeting adjourned."

Kerry, Tristan, and Melinda walked slowly back to Tristan's house. Kerry didn't quite know what to think. She did know she needed to figure out how she could be of help. The *John Coltrane*, with an empty cargo hold, could take as many as a hundred people, although they would be far from comfortable. She expected Galactic Central to send several colony ships, but it wasn't clear when that would happen. Kerry knew that she wanted to be one of the first ships out of the gate.

As they prepared dinner, they discussed the situation, and what should be done.

Tristan said, "I can pack up and be ready to leave in an hour. I don't need any of this stuff, really. All I need is a copy of House and a few things."

"We'll be packing them in on the John Coltrane, I expect, so it might not be pleasant for a while, love."

"It's OK, it will work out. I guess I get to think about where to head next much sooner than I thought."

Melinda said, "How will we get the colonists to leave?"

Tristan shook her head. "Short of landing colony ships and forcibly herding them on, I can't imagine."

Kerry said, "God, I hope it doesn't come to that."

House said, "Tristan, official word has come down from Galactic Central. Mandatory evacuation of all from Yagan City. They are scrambling big cargo ships and colony ships as fast as possible. The first ships will arrive in 24 hours; the full complement will likely take weeks. The colony leadership will determine the evacuation of colonists. Galactic Central will not give them a mandatory evacuation order."

Melinda said, "What? No! They can't do that! The priests will never allow it or tell the people of the danger!"

Tristan said, "Galactic Central thinks that colony autonomy is more important than lives, I guess."

Melinda said, "We must find a way to tell the people so they can choose for themselves."

Kerry said, "I understand, but we don't have a choice, Melinda. This is the order from on high."

Kerry could tell that Melinda was far from satisfied. But it didn't matter. Kerry had work to do.

"I need to head up to my ship, start preparations, and tell Galactic Central I have some space. I'd like both of you up there as soon as possible because I want the *John Coltrane* to be one of the first ships full and out of this system."

CHAPTER NINE

Several days later, Melinda was on her way to Luke's house. She was thinking about what was happening, and she was torn. She'd already decided she wanted to be on the John Coltrane, and Kerry had said that despite the chaos, she'd love to have her as an apprentice. Gaylin and Liana were apparently thrilled to get a systems assistant. The Galactic Central Evacuation HQ offered and accepted their evacuation slots, and the *John Coltrane* would be leaving in less than a week.

But she didn't want to just leave without doing what she could to spread the word to the colonists. She'd been expressing her frustration to Luke, who was gathering the banished at his apartment. She arrived at his door, and Gavin answered. They hugged.

"Hey Melinda, it's been a while."

"I've been busy lately with my studies, and now..."

"You're a little famous as the finder of the artifact."

"I know. It makes me a bit uncomfortable."

"Anyway, we're still waiting for the stragglers."

There were about ten people in the living room, so far, all of whom she knew, although a couple were less familiar to her than most. Finally, everyone had arrived.

Luke said, "Welcome, everyone. This is what we're here to talk about. Galactic Central has discussed evacuation with the priests, who, as we expected, refused evacuation. We need to do something, and all of you are here because you feel the same way I do. I've already declined my Evac slot on the first ship to help coordinate things."

Melinda remembered the shouting match between Luke and Tristan when he'd declined a spot on the *John Coltrane*. She thought he was endangering himself unnecessarily, and he felt she was being callous to the colonists' fate.

Gavin said, "I think we should take teams and go to each village and tell people what's going on and what their priest isn't telling them. That will allow them to make their own decision."

Luke said, "Galactic Central is prohibiting anyone from visiting the colonies."

Gavin said, "How can they prohibit it? There are about a dozen GC agents here, and they will be super busy, don't you think? We can take an air flyer. I'm willing to risk it."

There were nods around, and Melinda agreed. Why not? She said, "How can we get flyers?"

Gavin said, "I have access to them because of my job. They hold six. I can fly one. Let's start today--the sooner we get some colonists to Yagan City to get evacuated, the better!"

They gathered in teams, each covering ten of the fifty villages of the colonies. Each team had at least one member who had grown up in one of the villages they were going to visit, and they divided them geographically so that there was more chance some team members would talk to familiar people.

Melinda's team, which included Luke, would be first, leaving in a couple of hours. Gavin would meet the team in a large field on the outskirts of the city. Melinda wasn't going to tell Tristan what she was doing because she knew that Tristan would forbid her from going.

As she, Luke, and their team members walked to the field, they talked about what they thought they would find.

Luke said, "I don't think anyone will listen to us. The priests have so much sway. But it's worth a try."

Melinda nodded. It was worth at least a try. She didn't hold out much hope, but maybe if just a few could be saved, that would have been worth the effort.

They could see Gavin standing next to the flyer in the field, and they ran to meet him.

"Alright, folks, get in. Strap yourselves in when you sit down."

Melinda sat near the back next to a window and strapped in. She'd never been in a flyer before.

The flyer lifted gently off the ground and flew over the city's border into the country beyond.

"First stop, Chaceldon. Does anyone know anyone there?"

Joan, who grew up in the village next door said, "My sister lives there with her husband. We can start with her."

"Once we fly over the village, can you direct me to her house?"

"I think so."

As they were flying, Melinda saw this ramshackle-looking collection of houses with a square of rusty brown in the middle and realized she was looking at Chalcedon. She couldn't quite imagine that she'd come from a place like that--it didn't look real to her.

"Over there, see that big barn? That's my sister's place."

"Alright, we're going to land in her front yard."

As they landed, several people left the house and looked at the flyer with some degree of confusion.

"Joan, why don't you get out first?"

She did, and as Melinda was leaving the flyer, she watched her approach her sister, who looked panic-stricken.

"Joan?"

"Lydia!" They hugged.

"I didn't know what happened to you!"

A loud voice said, "What are you doing here?" It was a large man imposing himself between Joan and her sister.

"I'm here to tell you about a danger to all of you. There is an imminent attack on this colony, and there is a mandatory evacuation order. You must leave to save yourselves!"

He said, "I talked with the priest, and he was sure this was nonsense and a plot by Satan to rob us of our ability to follow God's will. We're not leaving. Go now and leave us in peace. Go back to where you came from."

Melinda said, "Do you realize that the city will be deserted? No one will be there?"

The man said, "That's a good thing."

Luke said, "No actually, it's not. No more seeds, no more vitamin C, no more vaccines. Even if the attack doesn't happen, you'll die here more slowly."

"God will provide. Get out of here, Satan!!"

He pushed Joan back, and when Luke went to protect her, the man punched Luke in the nose. Luke fell, with blood streaming from his face.

Gavin cried, "Let's get out of here!"

They went back into the flyer and took off. Melinda got the first aid kit and gave Luke some gauze to stem the bleeding.

Luke finally said with a nasal voice, "Well, that wasn't so successful."

Melinda nodded. "I hope some of the rest are better." But they weren't. They went to eight more villages, and each was the same. Gavin got shoved to the ground once, Melinda got slapped, and everyone was discouraged. The last village to visit was Revelation, her village. They landed in her old front yard. Her mother and brother emerged from the house.

"Mom!" She ran to her mother, and they hugged.

"Melinda! What are you doing here? If your father finds out you were here..."

"Mother, we are trying to warn people of the danger. They are evacuating this planet because of an imminent invasion. You have to leave to save yourself. And, if you don't leave, you'll die anyway because there won't be anyone to give you vitamin C or vaccines."

"Melinda, God will provide. I know it. I will follow what your father does."

"Mom!"

"Melinda, please leave now. Your father is due home any minute, and he will not want to see you here. Goodbye, Melinda."

"Mom!" Melinda's mother bodily pushed her away, and she finally turned and returned to the flyer. They stopped at Luke's family's house, and Luke barely avoided his father's shovel swing to his head. They flew back to the city, dispirited.

Luke said, "I thought it would be bad, but I had no idea it would be this bad."

A day later, the whole group was back at Luke's house. Every single team had had very similar results. No one agreed to come. The colony was going to die, one way or the other.

She had finally told Tristan what they'd done, and Tristan wasn't as upset as Melinda thought she would be. "I'm glad you told me afterward," she said.

The day before they were supposed to leave, they were making their final preparations when House said, "Melinda, you have been summoned to Galactic Central Evacuation HQ. Please leave immediately."

Tristan said, "I wonder what that's about? I think I should come with you."

Melinda nodded, and they left and walked to the administration building, which was now housing the evacuation effort. Someone behind a desk seemed to be fielding questions.

"Hi, I was summoned by Evac HQ."

"Name?"

"Melinda St. John."

He looked down. "Ah, yes. Please go to enforcement. That's office 231G."

"Thanks."

They walked up to the office and entered it to see all sorts of uniformed men and women scurrying around. Someone stopped and asked who they were.

"Melinda St. John."

"Oh, right. Please go into that room over there." She pointed to a door. They opened it, and it was a conference room. The group of them that had done the village visits were all there. She realized that they were probably in big trouble.

She greeted everyone, and they all looked worried. She and Tristan sat down. In a few minutes, a man who was not uniformed entered.

"Hello. My name is John Gracy. I want you to know that under ordinary circumstances, you all would be in a lot of trouble. Interference with colony affairs is something that we take extremely seriously. Several people wanted all of you in jail for a very long time to make an example of you. However, these are not ordinary circumstances; cooler heads understood what you were trying to do.

"We are not bringing any charges against you, but in return, we need your help."

Luke said, "Help?"

"Yes. It seems that your efforts paid off."

Melinda said, "What?"

"Approximately two thousand families have shown up so far to be evacuated, and it seems that many more are more coming."

Melinda and the whole group were stunned. Luke started to laugh, and it was infectious. They all laughed until John said loudly, "I don't at all see what is so funny!"

Gavin said, "If you had been there and experienced what we did, you'd be laughing, too. We were cursed, spat upon, slapped, punched, had things thrown at us, and were called Satan in more ways than I can count. The fact that we actually succeeded is frankly astonishing."

John nodded. "OK, I get it. Anyway, we need you to be our liaison with these people. They are very difficult to handle. We are placing a team of you in each ship that will evacuate the colonists."

Melinda realized that this was only fair. Based on her experience of being banished, the world these people were entering would be bewildering. Add to that the fact that they were rebelling against their priest, and they would be an unhappy lot.

"You'll get your assignments the next day, including who to report to and where. If you do not show up, you will be pursued and jailed. Do you understand?"

Everyone nodded. As Melinda and Tristan left the room and walked out of the building, they discussed the ramifications.

"It looks like we probably won't get to leave here on the *John Coltrane,* so your apprenticeship will have to wait until we can catch up to Kerry later."

"You're coming with me?"

"Of course I am. I'm responsible for you."

"But this is my fault. If I hadn't done this, you'd be leaving with Kerry. I don't want to delay you, and I know you want to be with Kerry."

"It's alright, really. We'll get off this rock and meet up with the *John Coltrane* at Wayfar, probably."

Melinda felt terrible and a little scared. Kerry's desire to leave the system as soon as possible was infectious, and Melinda felt it. But she knew she had no way of knowing when they would leave.

They got back to the house, and Tristan said, "House, please connect me with Kerry on the *John Coltrane*."

"Hey, Tristan."

"Hey love, a little snag."

"Snag?"

"Yeah. Remember that stunt I told you that a group of young people, including Melinda, did?"

"Um, yeah. Did they get in trouble?"

"Sort of."

"What happened?"

"They've been drafted to liaise between the colonists and the Evac system."

"Well, that makes a lot of sense. And you're staying with Melinda."

"Yeah, I need to."

"I understand. Pull strings, babe. Get an early ship, please? I have a bad feeling about this."

"I'll pull every string I've got. Luckily, I've collected plenty."

"I figured that. We expect to be out of here tomorrow. I'll call before we leave. I'll miss you."

"I'll miss you. We'll meet up soon, I promise."

Melinda still felt terrible, but she kept it to herself. This will work out, it will, she said to herself, over and over.

CHAPTER TEN

Kerry was in her quarters, pacing. She'd agreed, counter to her better wisdom, to carry Dr. Greenwald to Wayfar. He was late, and part of her wanted to leave without him, but she did feel some loyalty toward him. And besides, she couldn't leave because Ainsley was still on the surface with Shuttle One.

"Captain?" It was Abdul's voice.

"Yes, Abdul?"

"Ainsley called. She's en route with the Doctor."

Kerry felt relief. Now they could get underway, finally, and she could get the *John Coltrane* out of harm's way. She made her way up to the control room. Meadow, Abdul, and Liana were on duty.

"Are we ready to get out of here once Ainsely and Dr. Greenwald arrive?"

Abdul said, "Dr. Greenwald wants to speak with you."

"Patch him through."

"Dr. Greenwald?"

"Captain Jonas, thank you for speaking with me. I know you are anxious to leave the system…"

"Yes, Dr. Greenwald. We'll get in line for jump as soon as you are on board."

"I have authorization to give you first access to the jumpgate, as well as a hefty bonus, if you'll wait by it for a while."

"I don't understand."

"I've been given the go-ahead by Galactic Central to try to communicate with the aliens when they arrive in the Yagan system. I've been studying them my whole life, and I think we can communicate with them."

"Dr. Greenwald, this would put..."

"Captain, you would be in less danger than you are now. We would wait just next to the jumpgate. When they arrive, a transmitter on Yagan IV will try to communicate. The first sign that they either can't, or won't understand what we are saying, your ship can jump. It will be well before they get to the gate."

Kerry thought about it for a while. He was probably correct.

"Alright, I agree. When you get aboard, come to the control room."

"Thank you, Captain. I don't think you'll regret this."

Kerry hoped not. But she realized if she did regret it, she wouldn't have much time to experience that regret.

Kerry made her way back to the control room and sat in her chair, waiting for Ainsely and Dr. Greenwald to return. It made some sense to her that he might have gleaned a way to communicate with them from his years of study of the artifacts. And if they could communicate with them... at least they might understand more about their intentions.

Abdul said, "Captain, Shuttle One has arrived. Dr. Greenwald is on his way to the control room."

Eventually, Dr. Greenwald arrived.

"Dr. Greenwald, welcome to the control room. Strap yourself into that seat next to Abdul."

"Thank you, Captain." He maneuvered into the seat at the

spare station.

"So, what is the communications procedure?"

"We've set up communicators on Yagan IV, as well as satellites in orbit around Yagan V and VI, to send them a message with a lot of information, but which mostly says 'we're leaving, please don't shoot.' We hope this will at least buy us enough time to get everyone off of the planet."

"That sounds pretty reasonable. I hope it works. Meadow, put us in position 100 kilometers next to the jumpgate to Wayfar, please. Gaylin, have you gotten the authcode for priority jump access?"

"Yup, Cap'n. We're all set once we get into place."

Kerry said, "All there is to do now is wait."

In the meantime, ships came and went through the gate. Kerry was glad to see that the colony ships seemed to be arriving in good order. They waited about nine hours, then Abdul signaled that there was a lot of chatter on the jump gate channel. But there weren't as many colony ships as expected.

Kerry said, "Abdul, explain, please?"

"Several ships from that old species, the Dirilith, have just arrived through the gate."

"Aren't those the benefactors of the Korth?"

Dr. Greenwald said, "The benefactors of the benefactors of the Korth. They've been keeping to themselves for a very long time. I wonder what they are doing here now."

The ships went out further away from the jump point and Yagan IV. Kerry had no idea what was up, but she figured that a much older species than they were knew what they were doing.

A few hours later, after Kerry finally got some sleep, Abdul summoned her to the control room. She quickly got herself there and into her chair.

"Status?"

"Lots of chatter. The mystery ships have arrived in the outer system."

Dr. Greenwald said, "Abdul if you tune into channel z-alpha4, you should see indications that they've started the transmission to the aliens."

"Ah, yes, they have."

"Please monitor the channel for any response and record."

"Will do."

Gaylin said, "Putting the telemetry on the alien ships up on the display, Captain."

Kerry looked up to see a diagram of the system and the location of the alien ships. They had appeared first from somewhere around Yagan VI, approaching Yagan IV quite rapidly. Then, they appeared to be slowing, somewhat near the ships of the Dirilith.

"Am I seeing this right? Are they slowing down?"

Jaeden said, "They are that. Acceleration down to negative 1 kilometer/second squared. They should stop about 1 million kilometers outside of the orbit of Yagan IV."

Kerry felt some degree of relief. That meant something worked—either their transmission or the Dirilith, perhaps both.

Abdul said, "Dr. Greenwald, they are sending a response. I can't understand it, but I'm recording it."

"Gaylin, please send the stream to Dr. Greenwald's station."

"Done."

Kerry looked to see Dr. Greenwald hunched in his chair, looking intently at the display at his station. She could hardly imagine what he was seeing and what he might be doing. She imagined that he would probably study the response for the rest of his life.

"Dr. Greenwald?"

"I can't read all of this, but between the little bit I understand and the fact that they have stopped, it suggests that they will just leave us alone until we leave. Oh, wait. OK, yes, they will wait until... hmm... is that right? They will wait until their planet is cleansed of the... what? I'm not sure, but maybe it means 'unholy.' Well, anyway, they won't move until we're gone. It also seems they are a little angry with the Dirilith for some reason, but I can't tell what it's about."

"Their planet?"

"Yes, Captain, I've suspected for a while that this species used to inhabit this galaxy on the planets on which we've found artifacts. I'm getting the impression that we can communicate with them surprises them. I need to speak with the evacuation office. Can you patch me through?"

Abdul said, "Certainly, just a second." There was a pause. "Channel open."

"Dr. Greenwald?"

"Yes. We have communicated with the aliens successfully. They will wait until everyone is off of Yagan IV."

"We can't get everyone. The colonies..."

"You must force removal."

There was a long pause. "Affirmative. How much time do we have?"

"I can't say. The faster you can get it done, the better."

Kerry was glad the *Coltrane* was sitting next to the jumpgate with priority access, in case the aliens got impatient. But it seemed, from the hours they waited, and watched ship after ship leave the gate, and more arrive to ferry colonists, that the aliens would wait almost indefinitely.

"Captain, you might find this rather interesting."

"What, Abdul?"

"There is some very interesting chatter happening. Apparently three ships from that cult, 'The Gatherers,' entered the system."

"What?"

"What I said, Captain. It's weird. They are apparently on their way to the alien ships, right after the Dirilith!"

"Oh my God. They are crazy!"

Dr. Greenwald said, "Abdul, use code FG656 to get a priority override signal to those ships."

"Lead ship is the *Wilding*. Channel open, Doctor."

"Captain of the *Wilding*, this is Dr. Greenwald on behalf of Galactic Central. Do not engage with the aliens. You are endangering thousands of lives!"

"This is Captain McKale Simpson. They are not a danger to us, but we will wait until everyone is safe."

Dr. Greenwald said, "Thank you, Captain. Why are you approaching them?"

"They are the Ones we have been waiting for."

"Excuse me? They don't like human beings."

"They know us. We will be fine."

Dr. Greenwald muttered, "Crazy fuck." Everyone in the control room laughed.

Kerry was tempted to give that McKale Simpson a piece of her mind, but she refrained. At least she now knew the man actually existed. That whole incident with the hallucinogen still stung months later. But she knew he'd be dead soon, so it didn't much matter to her.

She needed another break. "I'll be in my cabin. Let me know if you need me."

As she sat in her cabin, looking over the communications chatter about the forced removal of the colonists from Yagan IV, she wondered how Tristan and Melinda were getting along. It was unclear where the colonists were being taken—no one seemed to know, and she imagined those who knew weren't telling. But it wasn't Wayfar, that much she could tell. She had no idea how long it would be before she got to catch up to them.

The next two days were nail-biting, but finally, the *John Coltrane* left, one of the last out of the system. Predictably, after all the ships that wanted to leave had gone, the aliens destroyed the jumpgate. Kerry didn't know the fate of the ships belonging to "The Gatherers," but she imagined it wasn't good. They dropped Dr. Greenwald off at Wayfar, which was chaotic and crazy. She still hadn't heard from Tristan, nor where the colonists had been taken, so she had to continue their work.

Her tablet kept a search on any mention of either Tristan or Melinda anywhere, and she kept hoping that she'd hear from Tristan at some point. She was awoken about a week after all of the events by her tablet.

"Kerry, mention of Melinda St. John and Tristan deSilva found."

"Explain."

"Galactic Court record, dated 2341 123.04.12. Melinda St. John was arrested at Dia V on suspicion of inciting a riot and assaulting an officer. Also being held on charge of interfering with an independent colony. Tristan deSilva, defense counsel."

Kerry asked her tablet, "Disposition?"

"Remanded into custody. Court date is not set. Court location Galactic Central Court."

Earth. They were on their way to Earth.

Kerry knew that Sevy, Liana, and Jaeden were on duty now. She punched the comm.

"Sevy, we're heading to Earth. How much will that shipment of feeder bolts get us there?"

"Uh, Captain, we'd have to pay to get rid of them. They are primarily used in deep-space hydroponics."

"What about the Moon?"

"Ah, the Moon. Lemme check."

"Meadow, set a course for Sol, please. We should be what, five jumps?"

"Exactly. I'm on it. Sevy, traffic?"

"Light all the way." A pause. "Oh, and you were sort of right, Captain. We won't make a huge profit, but we will make out halfway decently selling the bolts on Io. I've already got a potential buyer."

"You are amazing, Sevy! I'm going back to sleep now."

After dropping the bolts off at Io, they headed in-system to Earth. Kerry had declared shore leave of unknown length. She knew that Tristan and Melinda had made it to Earth, so Kerry was going to go find them.

CHAPTER ELEVEN

Melinda got her assignment. She'd be placed with Luke, Gavin and Joan on the cargo ship *Corinthian*, which had already arrived, and would be ready to load soon. Most of the residents of Yagan City had been evacuated already. Melinda seemed to think the name of the ship was auspicious. The families bound for the *Corinthian* were camping in one of the farm test fields, and they were supposed to start their work immediately, and live with those families now. She and Tristan took what they had and packed it on a cart. Tristan locked the door saying, "Not that I think I'll be back, but just in case."

They walked with the cart moving next to them out to the field. When they arrived, on one side was a large canopy, which looked to have food, water and supplies. They introduced themselves to the Evac crew.

"Hello, I'm Holden. Glad you've arrived. Set yourselves up over here, that's reserved for the liaison team." He pointed to an open space near the canopies. "This group is from Chaceldon, Revelation, Amos, Divinity, and Exodus. Hmm, that one is appropriate." He'd said them at first flatly, as if they had no meaning to him, but then Melinda could tell that he understood some things.

Tristan said that she'd get supplies and set up their camp. Melinda decided to go find people from Revelation, who were camped on the other side of the field. She doubted her family would be among them, since they were allied so closely to the priest.

"Melinda!" She saw her eldest sister waving excitedly.

"Kathy!" Apparently, her husband had decided that the danger warranted their leaving. They hugged.

"Mother refused to come, and dad threated Mike. I think that's actually what did it for him."

"I'm glad you are here. What about Tina?"

Kathy shook her head. "Her husband obeys the priest without question. So why are you here?"

"I've been made a liaison between the colonists and the evacuation crew. To make things easier. So, if anything comes up, find me. I'll be camped over there." She pointed.

"Well, we have everything we need. They have been very nice."

"We'll be on the same ship, so I'll see a lot of you. I'm glad you are here, Kathy. I need to walk around and visit with people."

"Can I come with you?"

"Sure, is it OK with Mike?"

"Oh, yeah, it will be fine. He's busy making himself a leader of sorts."

Melinda chuckled. That sounded like Mike. They walked around the area that her home village had been assigned to and saw many familiar faces. She was happy, now, that she'd done what she'd done. It had been for the best.

Later, she was sitting in the liaison camp with Luke, Gavin and Joan, all of whom had done rounds with people. Everyone seemed in good spirits about the whole thing.

Gavin said, "I heard they were going to place these folks on Jenkins."

Luke said, "That makes a lot of sense. Jenkins is a lot like

Yagan IV."

"And it's still pretty empty, apparently. I'll be happy to get this behind me. I have a job offer waiting on McKinney."

"I need to find a new medic training program that will take me. I'm heading to Berhend. Where are you going, Melinda?"

"I have a standing offer of an apprenticeship on the *John Coltrane*, with Captain Kerry Jonas. I don't yet know where I'll meet them, but they are currently on Wayfar. Joan, what are you doing?"

"I think I'll stick with these folks for a while. They'll need some help, and Galactic Central will certainly need some help with them. Then I'll figure out where I'll finish my training."

The next day, they got word that shuttle trips to the *Corinthian* would start immediately. The captain of the ship was anxious to get away. Everybody seemed anxious to get away. It would take many trips to get everyone off of Yagan into the Corinthian, and the liaison team was busy arranging who would go on which trip and smoothing ruffled feathers.

In the late afternoon, Melinda and Tristan had just gotten onto the shuttle with their stuff, when one of the shuttle crew ran to the door, shoved everyone out of the way, and closed it.

Tristan grabbed the man by the arm. "What do you think you are doing? Open that door! There are still people for this trip." That instant, the shuttle lurched, and they were launching.

"What's going on?"

"They're coming. Now! We have to leave! As it is, there are a few ships ahead of us at the jump gate. The captain said that if we didn't take off now, they would leave us."

Melinda was stunned. Her sister's family was on the other side of that door, as was Joan and Gavin. Luke had made it up on the first shuttle run. She didn't know what to think. She hoped that some other ships might be able to pick people up, but somehow, she doubted it.

They found seats and sat in silence for a long while. Melinda finally said, "I hope we can get out of the system in time. If we don't, I'm so sorry, this is my fault. If it hadn't been for me doing this, we'd be safely at Wayfar."

Tristan put her hand on Melinda's arm. "Don't be sorry. You did the right thing, even if I would have said you shouldn't do it. I'm glad you did, and even if I don't survive, there are hundreds of people who will because of you."

The shuttle lurched back and forth, then stopped, and Melinda got worried. But then the shuttle door opened again.

One of the crew walked back, and Tristan asked, "What happened?"

"We got a reprieve, apparently. The aliens are waiting for us to evacuate."

Melinda got up to go to the shuttle door and waited until she saw her sister. They hugged briefly, then Melinda got her and her family seats.

"We thought they would leave without us, and we'd be killed by the aliens!"

Melinda said, "Apparently they are waiting for us to leave."

"How nice of them."

Finally, the shuttle was full, and the door closed. After a while, then several bumps and shakes, a loud voice said, "Your attention please. We have just landed on the *Corinthian*. We will not be disembarking the shuttle until we are safely out of this system. Please remain where you are."

Everyone was getting restless. Melinda got up, and walked around, and talked with people, trying to calm them down. They'd never been in anything like this before, nor did they really understand what was happening. It was all new to them. The crew distributed water and food, and that helped some.

Later, the same loud voice as before said, "Your attention please. We have arrived at Wezlar. We are jumping directly to Dia, where there is a Galactic Refugee Authority camp on Dia V, where you will stay while being processed."

Melinda looked at Tristan. "Dia? I thought we were going to Wayfar?"

Tristan nodded. "Dia is pretty far from Wayfar. It will take us a while to get back to the *Coltrane*. We've got to figure out how to get word to Kerry that we're OK."

Tristan got up, and went toward the control area of the shuttle, but the door was closed. She knocked on it a few times. A haggard-looking man answered.

"Look, I need to get word to someone..."

"You and hundreds..."

"Look, these colonists..."

"I don't care. We're taking you to Dia V. I can't deal with you right now."

He shut the door in her face. She walked back to Melinda.

"No go. We'll have to figure something out when we get to Dia. She knows which ship we were assigned to, and I expect she'll be able to find out that ship made it out. But she'll worry about us until I can reach her."

There wasn't much to be done except wait. After more than thirty hours, the shuttle finally left the *Corinthian*, and landed on Dia V. The pilot came back, and the shuttle doors opened.

Dia V was the complete opposite of Yagan IV. It was as cool and wet as Yagan had been hot and dry. But it smelled bad to Melinda, like rotten eggs. It was almost overpowering. The shuttle had landed in a muddy field, surrounded by tall trees of a kind that Melinda had never seen before. She got cold as the mist around them started to stick to her clothes.

They walked toward a group of squat buildings that looked to Melinda to be made of a strange sort of material.

"Those are prefab units. I've seen a few on occasion, but we've not used them much on Yagan IV. They probably put them up here just to house the refugees."

They saw a few people approach them.

A tall woman with olive skin and long black hair tied behind her head said, "Hello, and welcome. This is one of the refugee areas we have set aside for you. There should be enough dwellings set up for all of the families that were on the *Corinthian*. Two other ships with colonists arrived earlier, and I know that several shuttles worth of colonists are still due from the *Corinthian*. You'll be placed in Section five."

Tristan said, "I'm Tristan, and this is Melinda. She's one of the liaisons, and I'm her foster mother."

One of the people, a short man said, "Ah, we have a building set up for the liaisons. Follow me."

As they followed him, Tristan said, "What about the refugees from Yagan City?"

"They were all sent to Wayfar."

"I don't understand, I thought we were all going to Wayfar, since the colonists were going to head to Jenkins."

The man paused a minute, then said, "You lived in the city?"

"Yes, as did Melinda. We both were brought up in the colony."

"I should tell you that Jenkins refused to take the refugees."

"What? But Jenkins is so similar to Yagan IV, and they have plenty of space."

"But their planetary council, representing all of the colonies on Jenkins, refused the placement of this colony there. It is their right."

"Why?"

"Are you really asking me that?"

Tristan sighed. "No, alright, fine. So, what's going to happen to these folks?"

"Galactic Central is working on it. That's all I know."

"Do you have interstellar messaging here?"

"Only for official business."

"I have someone I really need to contact."

"I'm sorry, but I can't help you at this time. Ah, here we are."

They had arrived at a prefab building and walked inside. On one side was a large lounge area, with chairs and couches. On the other was a few desks, and then behind that was a conference table, with chairs.

"And your housing is behind here..." They walked through the building, to a door in the back, and opened it, and there was a living room, kitchen and what looked like a few rooms off of a hallway in the back.

"You have five liaisons, I was told."

"Yes."

"There are actually six bedrooms back here, and a large bathroom. The plumbing isn't working yet, but we expect that to work in the next three to five days. There are portable bathrooms behind all of the buildings. There is a food distribution unit in the middle of the section, as well as a medical center. It will be your responsibility to process all of the refugees and send us a report of who is here in this section. Alright?"

Melinda nodded. He quickly left them, and Melinda felt bewildered.

She said, "What are they going to do when they find out there is nowhere to go?"

"They'll figure it out, Melinda, don't worry about it."

"Well, I should get back and help them orient."

Tristan said, "OK, I'll settle in here. See what I can figure out."

As Melinda entered the liaison office, she could already see people inside, waiting for her.

She asked, "Hi, have you found a place to stay?"

One man, who she'd met in the camp, came up to her.

"There is no well in the front of the houses."

"They don't use wells in the same way. There will be water inside the houses in about three days."

"So how do we get water now to bathe?"

"I'll find out. Just a moment."

She went to one of the desks that had a primitive interface. She had learned a lot and knew its capabilities almost immediately. It could take information, interact with the local network, and send messages locally.

She said, "System, please send a message to the coordinator that the refugees need a source of water for bathing."

A tinny voice said, at far too high a volume, "Acknowledged."

She looked up, and everyone was staring at her, and looking very jumpy.

She said, "Look, a lot of things are going to be unfamiliar. You'll get used to them. If you have any questions or needs, please ask me."

She fielded questions, answered the best she could, and asked the system to answer what she couldn't, although often it didn't know that anyway. Eventually, everyone filtered out of the office. She wondered where the other liaisons were, especially Luke. It would be nice to see him.

The official who had talked with them earlier came back into the office.

"I got your request for water. There will be no water except for drinking until we get the plumbing set up."

"That's three days?"

"Well, it's looking like it might be closer to five."

"They can't wait that long."

"They have to."

"You don't understand."

"What don't I understand?"

"They need to bathe."

"There won't be water for them to bathe for three to five days."

Melinda sighed.

"Bathing is very important to them."

"It doesn't matter how important it is."

"It's *holy*. Get it? Not bathing every day is a grievous sin."

He rolled his eyes. "You know where that comes from, don't you?"

"What are you talking about?"

Tristan, by now, had arrived back in the office. She said, "Look it doesn't matter. If you want this group of refugees to be happy, you *have* to find a way to allow them to bathe."

He turned to Tristan. "Look, we just can't do that. Yes, this is a wet planet, but the water here is so acidic it's toxic. We are waiting on a water treatment unit that is stuck at McKinney, and won't get here for at least three days. We only have bottled water, and just enough for people to drink 1 liter each a day."

"That little?"

"Yes. We... we didn't expect so many refugees. There is *no way*

I can help, here."

"What do you mean you didn't expect so many refugees? Why are we here? Dia isn't what anyone would call especially habitable."

"It's the best Galactic Central could do on such short notice. I have to tell you that there are many people who wished we'd just let that colony get destroyed by the aliens."

He turned and left. Tristan sighed. A group of more refugees entered the area near the liaison office, and Melinda saw Gavin and Joan. They hugged.

Melinda said, "Glad to see you!"

Joan said, "Good to see you too! What a trip, eh?"

Melinda nodded. "Let me show you our new digs."

Melinda went inside with Gavin and Joan, to show them their rooms. She returned to the office.

She said, "So what was that guy talking about, Tristan?"

"You never got around to reading that history of the colony, did you?"

"No, I never really wanted to."

"C'mon, sit down. Let's have a little chat. I think you need to know this now, given the situation. So, you've already learned that our little colony was started by this guy on Earth right after First Contact. Well, before First Contact, that guy, whose name was Pryor Alden, had a small church, with about ten families. They were notorious for protesting at funerals, and things like that, threatening the wrath of God because human beings weren't doing things right. No one paid them much mind, really.

"Then, First Contact happened, and Pryor, who was really just a sick guy with a serious opportunistic streak, said the kinds of things that people actually wanted to hear in the face of the huge confusion that was finding out that we really, really weren't alone anymore. At one time, his church, which became known as The One True Church about ten years after First Contact, had 400,000 members."

Melinda said, "400,000?"

"Yup. But that was before the Disaster."

"The Disaster?"

"Yes. Pryor, as I said, was a sick guy. And the core of his cult, that's what it is, was hatred of aliens."

"But we never learned about aliens."

"I know. That's because of the Disaster. Let me explain. He got his followers into such an anti-alien froth, that a group of them murdered a delegation of twenty-five visiting dignitaries from all over the galaxy, including six of the Korth."

"No!"

"Yes, Melinda."

Melinda put her head in her hands.

Tristan continued, "Most of his followers left the cult after that, but a core of about 10,000, except, of course, for the group that had murdered the delegation, and Pryor himself, who had been convicted of conspiracy, were allowed to leave Earth to create the colony on Yagan IV. It was one of the first colonies founded. The cult has changed a lot from when Pryor led it, but its nasty origins remain, even if changed, some. Remember what that official asked before about bathing?"

"Yeah, what did he mean?"

"The Korth live on a dusty dry planet, and they don't ever bathe, mostly because there is so little water on their planet, but also because the dust is protective to them, and it accumulates on them. They do have a way of tracking that dust from their bodies everywhere they go. Some humans find it gross. Proclaiming that bathing everyday was holy, and not bathing was a sin, was a way for the cult members to show their disdain for our benefactors, the Korth."

"That's horrible. I didn't know that."

"No one in the colony does. They've forgotten their history, probably on purpose. The priests probably know."

"I don't even know what to say."

"There isn't really anything to say, Melinda. I was just as horrified as you were when I found this out."

"Well, now I have the wonderful job of explaining to them why they can't bathe."

"It'll be OK, Melinda. I'll come with you."

They walked outside, and ran into Luke, who was on his way toward the liaison office.

"Hey, Melinda! Where's Joan and Gavin?"

"They are inside. They'll show you everything."

"Cool, I just got off the last shuttle on the *Corinthian*. They are heading out as fast as they can. The crew were not very nice to us. I don't really get it."

"I'll explain it sometime. Tristan just explained it to me. Look, we have a problem."

"What is it?"

"There won't be any water to bathe in for at least 3 days. The only water is 1 liter per person per day to drink."

"Oh, no! They will be very upset when they find out about that."

"I know. And we need to tell them now."

They walked to the central section, where the food distribution was, and they saw some agitated man and his wife berating one of the officials.

"I *demand* that you help us!"

"I'm sorry, but there is nothing I can do."

Melinda, Tristan and Luke walked toward them. Luke said, "Hey, Joey, take it easy. How can we help?"

Joey turned toward them. "You all probably don't bathe every day, since you are sinners. They won't help us get water for bathing."

Melinda said, "It isn't because they don't want to help. It's because they can't."

"There is plenty of water here!"

"It's toxic."

"What do you mean, *toxic*?"

"If you drink it, or bathe in it, you will get sick."

"That's just a lie you were told so that they could withhold water."

Luke said, "Joey, it's no lie, it's the truth."

"Why should I believe a bunch of *sinners*?" He stalked away.

Luke said to the official, "This is not going to be good."

The official laughed. "I don't care," he said, and he walked away.

It had been only two days. Two harrowing days. The colonists were getting increasingly belligerent at not having water, the conditions of their living spaces, not being given information, not having the proper food, and anything else they could imagine to complain about.

Melinda was tired and fed up. If it hadn't been for Luke, she would have demanded that the officials get them off this benighted planet. The planet was bad enough to deal with: horrible mud that ate away her shoes, the overpowering smell that only went away when the wind blew so coldly that everything froze, and she would get ice on her eyelids.

The living spaces were warm and comfortable enough, but everyone had to go outside to use the portable toilets, and get food, and it was miserable outside. She was also trying to finish up the census report—she thought that she and Luke had managed to finally make sure she had identified and processed everyone.

Tristan had had no luck in being able to contact Kerry, and Melinda knew that Kerry would be worrying about them. There wasn't anything she could do about it, so she just kept to the tasks she could.

She heard shouting outside of the liaison office. She turned to Luke, who also looked up from what he was doing. The shouting continued.

"I guess we'd better go find out what's going on?"

"Alright. Luke, I am so tired of this."

"Me too. I had no idea our people were such jerks."

They walked out together, to see a very large crowd of people outside the office, and Joey, who had emerged as the leader, shouting at an official, who stood cowering against the building.

"You have forced us to sin, and we will never forgive this. You are a tool of Satan..."

Luke interrupted. "Joey, look, it's not his fault that the water treatment unit got stuck somewhere in transit."

Joey shouted, "But it is their fault that we are here in the first place! We should have never left. They lied to us!"

"Look, Joey, calm down. The aliens did come."

"Liar!"

Joey turned to continue to shout at the official.

Melinda looked up to see even more people coming to join the crowd. Someone in the crowd started to shout "Satan! Satan! Satan!" at the official.

Melinda shouted, "Please be quiet!" She was drowned out by the crowd. At one point, she heard "They have batons!" on one side of the crowd. She squeezed her way through the crowd toward the new officials and faced a group of about thirty of them who were wearing helmets, and holding very large sticks.

She stood between the officials, and the crowd, who was shouting behind her.

"Look, please don't hurt them. They don't understand what's going on."

"Move out of the way!"

"Look, I'm one of the liaisons, I'm here to help. Let us deal with this."

"They have endangered one of our staff."

Melinda turned to the crowd. "Please, let him go. Let's just deal with this ourselves, OK?"

The crowd wasn't in the mood to listen to Melinda. They kept shouting. "Satan! Satan! Satan!" She shouted again, "Let's deal with this ourselves!"

The next thing she knew, she was roughly handled by one of the officials, and dragged away from the crowd.

"What are you doing? Leave me alone!"

She struggled with him. She felt a hard rap on her head, and she fell unconscious.

She woke up in a tiny room on a small bunk. She sat up and groaned. Her head hurt almost as bad as it did after the cave-in. She stood up and went to the door to open it. It wouldn't open. She tried several times, and it was clear that she was locked in. She looked back around the little room.

There was a small table with some water on it and a small, unidentified box in the corner. She opened the lid of the box to see a seat. Ah, the toilet. A small roll of toilet paper was on a little recessed shelf next to the toilet.

There were no windows, just light from the ceiling. She sat back down on the bed. She was locked up. She couldn't understand why. She had just been trying to help defuse the situation. She brooded.

She fingered her pendant, the one that she'd worn since her first week in Yagan City. It had been, for her, an emblem of her independence and that she'd gotten out of that colony. Now, it felt strange—it was an artifact from the species that took away her home. She left it on, but it weighed on her.

The door opened, and an officer walked in.

"Melinda St. John, you have a hearing."

She nodded, got up, and followed him. They went through some halls and finally came into a room where several officials were sitting and Tristan was sitting at a table with an empty chair. She motioned for her to come sit next to her.

Tristan whispered, "Let me talk, OK? Don't say anything. This isn't your trial, just a hearing. I'll explain it all later."

Melinda just nodded.

A man came into the room, and everyone rose, so Melinda followed suit. He sat at the desk that was slightly raised above the others.

"Alright, I don't want to spend any more time in this pit of a planet than I have to. Melinda St. John, please rise."

Tristan rose, and Melinda followed.

"You are charged with one count of assaulting an officer and one count of inciting a riot. How do you plead?"

Tristan said, "She pleads not guilty, your honor."

"And you are?"

"Tristan deSilva, Melinda St. John's council, your honor. Licensed at Yagan IV."

"Well, that's a shame, now isn't it? Since the plea is not guilty, there will be a trial, but there are no facilities here. And further, Earth wants you to stand trial for the charge of interfering with an independent colony."

Melinda said, "What?"

Tristan put her hand on Melinda's arm. "Excuse her, your honor; she is unfamiliar with court protocol. Why is this charge being brought? It was my understanding that in exchange for her service as a liaison, those charges would not be filed."

"According to Earth, those services were not fulfilled."

Melinda groaned.

Tristan said, "I see."

"What is her plea?"

"She pleads not guilty to that charge as well."

"Melinda St. John is to be remanded to Galactic custody and transported to Earth for trial. Are you going to accompany her?"

"Yes, I will, your honor."

"You are both leaving on the ship that brought me from Diallo. It is leaving in one hour."

Tristan turned to Melinda and said, "Don't worry, kiddo. It will be fine. I promise. I'm a damn good lawyer."

Melinda smiled. "That doesn't surprise me."

"I knew we'd be leaving with the judge. Our stuff is already packed. I'll get it on that ship. I'll see you soon."

An officer stood next to her. She got up, and he put metal bracelets on her hands and ankles. She imagined they prevented her from going far or doing much, so she didn't bother to test them. She was led back to her cell, and she paced for a while until someone else arrived and led her outside to the landing pad.

This shuttle was much larger than any she'd seen before. She was led onto the shuttle, and briefly saw Tristan before she was led to the back into a small compartment.

"If you need the bathroom, knock on the door. Otherwise, just stay in here. Please strap in, we will be at low gravity."

Melinda nodded, and the door closed. She strapped herself into the seat.

The compartment had a nice window, at least, so she watched as the shuttle took off, and she could see the landscape of Dia recede as the planet's curvature became obvious. Relatively soon, the planet itself began to recede into the distance. Dia's sun wasn't visible, and it was hard to get a sense of how fast they were moving. Melinda got lost in thought.

She wasn't sure what was going to happen on Earth. She hadn't had a chance yet to talk with Tristan, so she had no idea what she was facing. She remembered that John Gracy had said that there were people who wanted to put them in jail for a long time for telling the colonists about the danger. And she had no idea how serious the charges of "inciting a riot" and "assaulting an officer" were. She did know that Tristan would do everything she could to make sure that Melinda didn't end up in prison.

She looked up when she saw the shuttle fly relatively close to some sort of structure in space. It was like a column of some sort and went as far above and below as she could see. She then realized it was a ring, and they were flying through it. She thought, "Oh! A jump gate."

The shuttle shuddered a little as they flew through, but nothing else. Once the ring went by her window, there was nothing else to look at for a while except the canopy of stars. She brooded. She wondered what her life would be like if she had to spend time in prison. It wasn't fair! She had just been trying to help—help save lives and help calm people down. She shook her head. So much for getting to learn the spacer trade or explore the galaxy.

The shuttle was passing relatively close to the moon, and then she saw Earth. It looked exactly like she'd seen it when shown by House. Blue and brown, with lots of white swirls. She hoped that at least she'd get to see some of Earth, but she had no idea how much.

The shuttle approached this very strange-looking large platform tethered to the planet with a long, gossamer thread. She realized that it was one of the space elevators she'd read about recently. As they approached it, she realized how large it was. It appeared that they were going to land on it, somehow. The platform got larger and larger, until she could no longer see the edge of it through her window. There was a small bump, and then the shuttle began to descend, as if on an elevator, down through the platform. The shuttle eventually stopped moving.

The officer who had put her in the compartment opened the door.

"We're here. Please follow me."

She undid the straps and followed him out of the shuttle. She didn't see Tristan. She was flanked by four officers, and they walked down hallways, and then entered into a large space where there were a lot of people. She could see Tristan in a group of others, but they did not approach them.

She observed her surroundings. It was a large space, with tall ceilings, and large windows all around, with a view of Earth. There were some stores and restaurants, and there was a large waiting area, with seats. It was a circular space, with the center of it being largely obscured by tall walls. She assumed this was where the elevator cars loaded and unloaded.

She'd learned that about 100 years ago, Earth decided that it didn't want shuttle or ship traffic taking off and landing on Earth, so they constructed a series of ten space elevators. Shuttles would land on the platforms, and people and cargo would be moved via the elevators.

"C'mon, come this way."

She followed the officers through the large area to the center. People were staring at her, pointing, and murmuring to their companions. She didn't know whether they knew who she was, or whether they just stared and pointed at everyone who was in custody. They entered into some sort of wide hallway going deeply into the center, at the end of which was a set of doors. The doors had red lights around them.

Melinda looked to her side to see Tristan standing about 5 meters away. Tristan smiled at her, and she smiled back. The lights around the doors became yellow and flashed. Finally, the doors opened, and the lights turned green.

"Follow me."

Melinda followed the officer into the elevator. He led her to a seat.

"Sit here. Please don't move."

She nodded. She had no intention of doing anything rash. Eventually, the elevator began to descend. It was a stunning view, and she enjoyed it for the entire hour it took to get to the surface. She knew that there were actually four elevators on each cable, and they were only on one. It was large and looked like it could carry a hundred people. But this elevator clearly had been reserved for their party. There were officers, the judge, some assorted officials, Tristan and herself.

The elevator finally came to rest, after it had gone below the surface. She got up, and followed the officer out, and through the terminal space. She was led to a small vehicle without windows. She had no idea where they were going, but soon enough, she was led through some more corridors, and through large metal doors, and finally to another small cell.

The officer removed the bracelets around her wrists and ankles and closed the door.

This cell was a bit larger than the one she'd been in on Dia. It had a sink with running water, a real toilet, and a comfortable bunk. She relieved herself, and then took a nap.

"Melinda St. John." Her eyes snapped open. She said, "Yes?"

"You have a meeting scheduled with your counsel in ten minutes."

"Thanks."

Melinda got up and washed her face. The door opened, and a woman officer stood there.

"Come with me."

She was eventually led to a room with a table and two chairs across from each other.

"Sit."

She sat. The officer left. The door opened, and Tristan, followed by an officer, came in. Tristan sat.

"How are you, Melinda?"

"I'm alright. Confused, scared, but alright, I guess."

"We'll get you out of this, I promise. The charges are bogus, and even they know it."

"So, what do we need to do?"

"Well, the trial date hasn't been set yet. It could take a few weeks for that to happen."

"A few weeks? Oh, man. I am going to get so bored!"

"Actually, your cell has a system, and you are allowed a tablet."

"I am?"

"Yes. Of course, what you do is carefully monitored, and you can't contact the outside world. I'm working hard to get permission to move the copy of Dr. Porter's system here so you can keep working on your studies. But I can't guarantee that. They are in a foul mood."

"A foul mood?"

"Well, the alien attacks have been a horrible blow to the galactic economy, and it reminded everyone of The One True Church, so people are looking for someone to blame."

"Me? Wait, if it hadn't been for me, everyone in Yagan City would be dead now! Let alone the colonists."

"I know, Melinda, I know. It's not rational."

"So those people we saw, who stared and pointed—they know who I am?"

Tristan nodded. "You are getting famous. The trial is likely to be 'casted everywhere."

Melinda sighed.

"But Melinda, really, don't worry. I'm a damn good counsel, and I've got a great list of witnesses for the trial. Oh, and Kerry is on her way."

Melinda smiled. "That's nice. I'm glad she knows we're OK."

"Me too."

The officer that brought her came back into the room, and bellowed, "Time's up!!"

Tristan held Melinda's hand. "You'll be alright, I promise."

Melinda could feel the tears in her eyes. Her throat tightened. She could only nod.

The officer pulled her arm, and Melinda rose, and left the room, going back to her cell.

"Do you know when I can get a tablet?"

"It's in there now."

"Thanks."

The officer opened the door, and Melinda entered the cell. The door closed behind her. She fell to her bunk and cried.

CHAPTER TWELVE

Kerry walked down the street of this ancient city. She'd been to New York once or twice before, and she'd never really enjoyed it, although she knew that it was a galactic tourist destination. It was the seat of the Galactic human Government, and, slowly, but surely, all of the other functions of the city had gone elsewhere, until nothing was left except the government.

She and Tristan had finally had a chance to communicate once Tristan made it to Earth. Tristan had rented an apartment, since the length of time she would have to stay was indeterminate. Kerry didn't envy Tristan the job of defending Melinda in the current climate, but she knew that Melinda probably had the best person for the job.

She walked down 14th street, and found the building Tristan was in. It was very quiet in New York these days. She remembered reading about the loud, bustling city that it used to be, but there really weren't any loud, bustling cities anywhere anymore, now that humanity was spread all over the galaxy.

She walked to the entrance, and after a short while the outer door opened for her. She walked up the stairs, and Tristan was standing in a doorway. Kerry ran to her, and they embraced tightly.

"I was *so* worried about you, love."

"I know. I'm so sorry I couldn't get word to you sooner. It's been a nightmare. C'mon in."

Kerry walked in and closed the door behind her. She dropped her bag and followed Tristan to the one couch.

"This place isn't so well furnished. But what sold it was that it has a class five system. I need that."

"Class five. Wow."

"Yeah. The owner of the place is some sort of artifical intelligence fanatic. I'm happy."

"How's Melinda?"

"Hanging in. I've seen her a few times. She's confused and scared she might spend the rest of her life in prison."

"Is that a possibility?"

Tristan nodded. "If she's found guilty of all three counts, the minimum she'd get is thirty years, likely working in the asteroid belt."

"Ugh. But the charges..."

"Are completely bogus. So, I have to prove it. The problem is..."

"They want to hang her. I know. I've been watching the news and analysis shows. It's crazy."

"That theory that it's TOTC's fault that Rigel was destroyed..."

"That's crazy. In fact, I finally heard from Dr. Greenwald — you'd never believe the true story."

"The true story?"

"Yeah. Remember I told you about the Dirilith ships that arrived at Yagan?"

"Vaguely. It's been crazy time, Kerry."

"Anyway, it turns out that the benefactors of the Dirilith…"

"Like our great-grand-benefactors?"

"Right! Anyway, they had promised to safeguard the sites so they didn't get settled, while this other species went off to explore another galaxy."

"Oh, really?"

"Yeah. And that species figured that when it found the systems empty of that guardian species…"

"They assumed something bad had happened."

"Right."

"But it turns out the Dirilith benefactors just died out. The Dirilith aren't sure why. And the Dirilith had vaguely known of the promise, but didn't know what planets were supposed to be guarded, so…"

"Wow."

"It was like hundreds of thousands of years ago, apparently."

"Well, I guess it's nice to know it won't happen again."

"Not like it did. But there are six more systems that need to be evacuated, two populated by humans."

"Oh, man."

"Yeah, it's bad. Anyway, when does the trial start?"

"The date hasn't been definitely set. Likely, though, it will start sometime next month."

"I'd like to stay here."

"Kerry, your business…"

"Is moribund. The economy has cratered, and it's a good time to take a long sabbatical anyway. My entire crew wanted a good long break, and so I'm giving it to them. I figure we'll be fine for three months. After that, I'll probably have to go make some money. Besides, I got a bonus for helping at Yagan IV, and thanks to your persuasive arguments, I not only got my entire fine for that silly bogus shipment reimbursed, but I got a nice little settlement on top for pain and suffering. Thanks, babe."

Tristan smiled, and crawled on top of Kerry, pinning her down.

She kissed her.

"Show me how much you are grateful."

The next few weeks were a blur of Tristan preparing for trial, visits with Melinda, and a few nights out for the two of them, to take their minds off of what was happening. The court date was set. Tristan still didn't know which judge would be assigned to the case.

Finally, one day, Tristan was preparing her opening arguments, while Kerry was doing some research, when the apartment's system, in its light, pleasant voice said, "Tristan, the judge has been assigned to the case. Her name is Katerina Nora. Shall I give you a summary?"

"Please."

"She was born on Earth in 2295 and has spent her whole career in the Sol system. She was a United States provincial district prosecutor and became a judge in 2335. She is generally considered a conservative judge, favoring longer sentences than average."

"Any opinions on record about colonial autonomy?"

"Yes, one. She ruled in favor of Galactic Central and against the Salinas colony on Jenkins IV, around their policy of refusing vaccinations."

Kerry said, "That's good, right?"

"Yes, love, very good."

"Any connections to The One True Church?"

"Negative."

"Any opinions related to cults?"

"No."

"Thank you."

Tristan was hopeful. Yes, it was a conservative judge, but one that was flexible when it came to colonial autonomy issues, at least as they related to health and safety.

"Well, I guess I'm just about as prepared as I can be for the trial start next week, Kerry. I've got the petition to separate the charge of interference with a colony from the other charges, and strategies for whichever direction the judge chooses. I've got a great line up of witnesses, and I've been prepping Melinda. She'll be ready."

"How have you been prepping her?"

"To be herself, but more of it."

Kerry smiled. "Yeah, that sounds about right."

"I've explained that she needs to show her honesty, and her smarts, and the deep conflict she has with TOTC. To explain what she risked even though she hated the life she'd left. But she cared about the people. She has to be seen not as a member of TOTC, but a rebel. She's fine with that."

"When are you putting her on the stand?"

"Last. She'll be the last witness."

"What kind of witnesses do the prosecution have?"

"Not many that are especially useful. There are the officers who were at Dia, John Gracy, who I think will not be as useful as they think. Plus, a long list of expert witnesses who will testify about TOTC. I can't tell you how much I am looking forward to cross-examining them!"

"And you have?"

"Josh, Luke, Dr. Greenwald, Dr. Porter, Dr. Boomer, an expert witness on children of cults, and Melinda herself."

"Not me?"

"No babe, conflict of interest."

"I get that. Well, I certainly am looking forward to watching. I got my tickets."

"That I helped with." Tristan smiled.

The morning of the trial Melinda paced in her cell. She'd been prepared for weeks, now, and she was ready to just get this over with. Tristan had said that the trial might take weeks. She was confident in Tristan, but she worried, nonetheless.

Tristan had gotten her some nice clothes to wear at the trial: a white shirt with beautiful azure blue buttons, black pants made of silk, and some nice, and comfortable brown shoes. Tristan told her to wear the pendant. She worried about that a little, but she paid attention to Tristan, and put it over her head.

The door to her cell opened, and an officer stood outside the door. She left her cell, and followed the officer through corridors and up elevators, and finally to a large room that was filling with people. She was taken to the large table with Tristan sitting at it. She sat down next to her and looked around.

The room was a semicircle, with a raised platform and a large desk at the front, a Galactic Central flag on one side, and a flag she didn't recognize on the other side. To the side were two rows of chairs that were currently empty. Behind the two desks, one of which they sat at, and the other that she assumed had the prosecutors, were rows of seats that were now filling up. She assumed these were for the spectators.

"Melinda!" She heard a loud whisper behind her. She turned around to see Kerry's smiling face. She smiled and waved.

"Hi Kerry. Good to see you!"

Tristan put her hand on Melinda's arm and bent toward her.

"You shouldn't speak again, OK?"

Melinda nodded, becoming serious again. Things settled down in the room, and at one point a line of people came through one of the doors and sat in the row of seats in the front.

Melinda whispered to Tristan, "Is that the jury?"

Tristan nodded. "Don't stare, don't smile, and don't react to them, OK?"

Melinda nodded again.

A man in a suit at the front of the room said, "Please rise."

Everyone stood. The judge, who was a diminutive woman, with brown hair and wearing a strange-looking robe walked into the room and sat at the desk in the front.

"Please be seated."

There were exchanges of legal conversation that Melinda could not follow. It had something to do with separating the charges. The final result seemed to be that she would be tried for all of them during this trial. Finally, it was time for the prosecution to give their opening argument. Tristan had reminded Melinda that she could show her emotional responses—she should not appear impassive to the arguments brought against her.

"Your honor, members of the jury, we are here today to bring serious charges against Melinda St. John, member of The One True Church."

Melinda was shocked. She had been banished, and besides, she would never have considered herself such. She sighed.

"We will show that Melinda purposefully circumvented regulations to warn members of her church of the impending alien attack, that she incited a riot once the church had been settled on Dia V and attacked an official who was just trying to help the best he could. These were malicious acts, intended to further the aims of The One True Church, and she should be punished to the fullest extent of galactic law for these offenses."

Melinda was angry, and balled her fists, her nails biting into her palms. She shook her head. The prosecutor went on, but she didn't really hear much of what he had to say. She could feel the tears flowing down her face.

Tristan rose, and Melinda realized it was her turn to speak.

"Your honor, members of the jury, the defense will show that Melinda is not a member of The One True Church, and never tried to further its aims. She was raised knowing nothing but the church, hated living in it, and was banished from it for her independent spirit. Nonetheless, when she learned of the impending alien attack, and knew that the priests of the church would not let the people leave, she, and other brave banished people, gathered together to try and save as many innocent women and children from the alien attack as she could.

"Later, on Dia, she was doing her best to be the liaison she had been forced to become, and in the process, she was wrongly accused of inciting a riot, and assaulting an officer. She has always been cooperative. The defense will conclusively show that Melinda is an innocent who was doing her best, not the malicious church member the prosecution would like to paint her as."

The judge said, "The prosecution may call its first witness."

The prosecutor said, "Thank you, your honor. We call Officer Chuck Klayton."

Melinda watched the officer walk into the room and sit in a chair near the judge. She didn't recognize him.

"Do you swear to tell the truth, subject to charges of perjury?"

"I do."

"Name and assignment, please?"

"Officer Chuck Klayton, assigned to Dia V Resettlement Camp."

"Describe for me please the events of 2341 122.14.04?"

"We had been alerted that a group of church members were surrounding one of the resettlement officials, and a group of us went to try and disperse the crowd. When we arrived, there was a lot of shouting, and we could see the official was in danger."

"Did you see Ms. St. John?"

"Not immediately. But as we approached, and people began to realize we were there, she pushed through the crowd, and got between us."

"And then what happened?"

"She shouted 'Let's deal with this ourselves,' and then came toward us. The crowd followed her. I grabbed her to arrest her, and she struggled and hit me several times. I finally managed to disable her. The crowd went nuts, and it took us almost a half hour to disperse the crowd."

"So, you would say the crowd was following her lead?"

"Most definitely, sir."

"Thank you. No further questions."

Tristan rose and walked toward the officer.

"Officer Klayton, did you know that the colony on Yagan IV have no police?"

"Excuse me?"

"Did you know that the colony on Yagan IV have no officers? And there are very few officers in Yagan City?"

"No, I didn't know that."

"So, neither Melinda, nor the colonists, would understand your authority, because they had never been exposed to it. Does that change how you look at what happened?"

"Well..."

"Might you say that if they had no idea why you were there, they might react similarly to a crowd that knew why you were there but were being belligerent?"

"Yes, they might... but..."

"But what, officer?"

He was silent, then shook his head.

"And might it make sense for an individual to struggle, who had no experience with officers?"

He said very quietly, "Yes."

"Excuse me?"

Louder, "Yes."

"No further questions, your honor."

"You may step down, Officer Klayton."

Melinda watched him, and he seemed almost reluctant to leave the stand. It was clear that what Tristan had said had shaken him, and it seemed that it had changed the feeling of the entire room.

"The prosecution's next witness is John Gracy."

John walked into the room and sat in the chair. He was introduced, and sworn in.

"Mr. Gracy, explain how you discovered that a group of The One True Church members had circumvented regulations, and flown to the colony villages to try and get people to leave?"

"There had been some chatter in the security offices of unauthorized flights into the colony, but no one knew who it was. Later, when colonists began to show up in Yagan City, we asked them how they had heard, and they identified seven people, all members of the church, living in Yagan City."

"Your honor, please add into evidence the flight record of the flyer that was identified as the one that went several times into the colony."

"Accepted."

The prosecutor turned back to John. "What happened next?"

"We called those people in."

"And did you arrest them?"

"There was some clamor to do so, but we decided that they

were better used as liaisons, to help with the colonists."

"How did that go?"

"Not very well. They didn't really do as they were told, and things, as you've heard, got out of hand."

"No further questions, your honor."

Tristan rose. She had told Melinda that she knew John personally. She thought this might be very interesting.

"John, when you called those people in, how quickly did they arrive?"

"Um, immediately."

"So, they obeyed your call to come in? They fully cooperated with you?"

"Um, yes."

"You mentioned a clamor to arrest them. What was the reasoning?"

"Well, as you know, Tristan, colonial autonomy is given the highest priority."

"Is it?"

"Yes. Some people felt that we should make an example of them."

"An example?"

"Yes."

"I see."

"You were in charge of the effort to tell the colonists about the attack threat, were you not?"

"Yes, I was."

"Whose decision was it to only inform the priests?"

"Um, that came from the very top."

"Before this incident, what was your job?"

"I led the committee on Yagan that was tasked with the colony's welfare."

"I see. You are quite familiar with The One True Church, then are you not?"

"Yes."

"Would you say that the absolute rule of the priests is a hallmark of the cult?"

"Yes."

"So, what did you think the likelihood that priests would communicate the threat to others in the church?"

There was a pause.

"John?"

"Nonexistent."

"And what did you think the likelihood was that the priests would decide to leave Yagan given the information you shared with them?"

Another pause, this time, longer. Tristan let it go.

John finally said quietly, "None."

"I see. So, in your judgment, would the decision from the very top, to only inform the priests, result in the elimination of The One True Church when the aliens attacked?"

Melinda could see him squirm.

"Yes, it would."

Tristan said, "And would you say that was the intent of the decision in the first place?"

The prosecutor rose forcefully and shouted, "Objection! Calls for conjecture."

The judge said, "I agree with that objection. Counselor, move on."

"John, are you familiar with the story of Hatsimon VI?"

He was quiet a moment, then said, "Yes."

"Tell me about it?"

"Hatsimon VI had a small, very insular colony on it. It was removed by Galactic Central."

"Why?"

"Because there was too much volcanic activity. Several volcanoes were in imminent danger of engulfing the colony."

"Did they ask permission to remove the colony?"

"No."

"Did the colonists want to leave?"

"No."

"They just forcefully evacuated the colony?"

"Yes."

"So colonial autonomy was suspended in the face of certain destruction in that case?"

"Yes."

"Why didn't Hatsimon VI serve as a model for Yagan IV?"

"Well, it did. We did forcefully remove the colonists."

"But not at first, only after the aliens arrived and forced your hand. I ask again, why didn't Hatsimon VI serve as a model for Yagan IV?"

"I can't say, I didn't make the orders."

"Alright. Thank you, John. No further questions."

The judge said, "It's time for a recess. We will reconvene in one hour."

Melinda and Tristan sat in a room off of the courtroom. Kerry brought them lunch, but she couldn't be in the room with them.

Melinda said, "Wow, Tristan. Two witnesses up, two down! You are doing great!"

Tristan smiled. "They are making it too easy, Melinda. I'm just showing these charges for what they are."

The trial continued for days. The prosecution had a long line of witnesses speaking of the dangers of The One True Church. Tristan picked them apart, one by one. In the end, Melinda didn't think that either side won that one decisively. Those already inclined to hate TOTC wouldn't have been swayed, but those who were more willing to be open-minded wouldn't have been swayed either.

One exchange was particularly interesting. It was an expert witness who had supposedly studied the Yagan IV colony, but in fact, didn't really have a clue about it.

Tristan was cross examining. She said, "You said in your testimony that all cult members obey the priests absolutely at all times, and if they don't that is punishable by death."

"Yes, that was one of our findings."

"And are you aware that cause of death is required to be recorded by the colony and sent to the Yagan committee for every death?"

"Er, no, I wasn't aware of that."

"And also, that colonial autonomy means that execution is allowed."

"Well, of course."

"Your honor, I bring into evidence the census records of the colony on Yagan IV over the past fifty years."

"Accepted."

"Over the past fifty years, there have been approximately 20,000 deaths in the colony. 85% of those deaths were people over the age of 45, and 13% were people under the age of 10. Only 2% of deaths were in people from the ages of 10 to 45, and all of those were listed as accidents. Why would the colonists lie about this?"

"I don't have an answer."

"Is it possible that the punishment is not in fact death?"

"Well..."

"Is that possible?"

"Well, I guess so."

"Your honor, I bring into evidence the citizenship records of Yagan IV, showing 469 individuals separated from the colony for reasons of unsuitability. One of whom is Melinda St. John."

"Accepted."

"No further questions."

Melinda knew that Tristan was setting something up, ready for her own witnesses.

Finally, it was time for Melinda to take the stand. She was ready to get this over with.

"Do you swear on penalty of perjury, to tell the truth?"

"I do."

She sat down, and watched Tristan approach her.

"Name and last position, please?"

"Melinda St. John, Liaison to Yagan IV colonists."

"First, Melinda, I want you to explain why you were banished from the colony."

"I got caught exploring, among other things."

"Other things?"

"I didn't want to get married, I disobeyed the priest once, and..."

"Keep going."

"I got caught with a girl."

There was a laugh in the room.

"I see. You were banished when you'd been injured in the cave in—the one where you found the artifacts?"

"Yes."

"Were you happy to be banished?"

"Oh, yes. I was going to run away anyway, but this turned out to be much easier."

"Once you were banished, did you miss the colony?"

"God, no! I hated it there!"

"What about your family?"

"I missed my mother a little. And I missed my older sister Kathy a lot."

"So, when you found out about the potential attack, what did you think about the plan that only the priests would be told?"

"I knew it meant that no one would be allowed to leave. The priests would say it was some sort of plot, and wouldn't tell the people, so they couldn't decide for themselves."

"And you wanted to do something about it?"

"Yes! Why should thousands of innocent people die because some guys wanted to keep hold of their power? It wasn't fair!"

"Melinda, when you were growing up, had you ever heard of aliens?"

"No. I knew we weren't on the planet that we used to be on."

"How did you learn that?"

"I snuck books from my father's library. Women aren't supposed to read."

"Really? Women aren't supposed to read? How did you learn?"

"My mom taught me. She'd been taught, and she thought I should learn. I learned a lot more than she taught me, though."

"By borrowing books you weren't supposed to read?"

"Right."

"But there were no mentions of aliens?"

"No, not any."

"So, when you were told about the Disaster, how did you feel?"

"Horrible! I felt terrible. I couldn't believe that my people were the cause of that!"

"Would you think it likely that most people in the colony have no idea the Disaster happened?"

"Maybe the priests know, but I overheard enough conversations with my father and other men, and nothing like it was ever mentioned."

The questions continued, and they were easy to answer. Tristan asked about her perspective of what happened on Dia, and other things. Finally, she was finished. It was time for the cross-examination.

"Melinda, did you know about the regulations regarding interference with colonies before your group did its work trying to tell the colonists?"

"Yes."

"So, you knew you were circumventing regulations?"

"I felt that there were serious extenuating circumstances."

"And you took it on yourself to assume that, rather than leaving it up to the Galactic officials?"

"The Galactic officials were going to let everyone on the colony die. We couldn't let that happen."

"So, you took it on yourself to circumvent the regulations? Yes, or no?"

"Yes."

"No further questions, your honor. The prosecution rests."

The judge said, "Counsel?"

"The defense rests, your honor."

"We will reconvene tomorrow for final arguments."

The next day, Tristan and the prosecutor gave their closing

arguments. Not so different from the opening ones. The jury then was sent out for deliberation, and Tristan and Melinda were sitting eating lunch, waiting.

"Tristan, how do you think it went?"

"I think it went about as well as it could have. I have to tell you, Melinda, there is a chance that you will be found guilty of interference."

"Yeah, I figured that."

"But I'm hoping this judge will be lenient. She's got some wiggle room, I think."

Melinda was silent. She found it oddly ironic that she might go to prison for trying to save her people—people she'd been happily banished from.

The door opened, and someone said, "The jury is back."

Tristan looked shocked. "Already?"

They got up and went back into the court room. When they sat down, Melinda said, "What does this mean, Tristan?"

"It's either very good news, or very bad news, Melinda."

That didn't sound good at all to Melinda. The jury filtered in, and then they all rose for the judge.

She said, "You have come to verdicts to all three charges?"

One of the jury members said, "We have."

"Please tell us."

"On the charge of inciting to riot, we find Melinda St. John, not guilty. On the charge of assaulting an officer, we find Melinda St. John not guilty. On the charge of interference with the autonomy of a colony, we find Melinda St. John guilty as charged."

Melinda felt the fear in the pit of her stomach. She had no idea what to expect next.

The judge said, "Thank you for your service. You may be dismissed."

She turned to Melinda. "Melinda, please rise."

Melinda rose.

"I have been given a very difficult task, young woman. The jury has found you guilty of a very serious charge. But it seems cruel to put you in prison for your desire to save lives, since it has been made clear that was your only aim. And it is also clear that precedent was not followed initially on Yagan IV, precedent that would have forced the removal of the colony."

There was a pause. Melinda held her breath, and she could feel Tristan's hand on her arm.

"I would like to sentence you to probation, but I am not able to, because you currently have no home, nor gainful employment, since you have been officially severed from your liaison duty. Those are requirements for a sentence of probation."

Melinda raised her hand.

"Yes?"

"I have gainful employment, and a home, your honor. I was accepted to be an apprentice with Captain Kerry Jonas, on the ship *John Coltrane*, before the incident. Is that what you had in mind?"

The judge smiled. "Is Captain Jonas present?"

Kerry stood. "Yes, your honor."

"Is this so?"

"Yes, your honor."

"Are you willing to oversee Melinda's probation?"

"With pleasure, your honor."

"Alright then. Melinda, you are sentenced to eight years' probation. Please report to the probation authority on Ganymede before you leave the system."

"Yes, your honor."

"This court is adjourned."

Tristan gave Melinda a big hug. "It's over!"

"I feel relieved. And I don't have to go to prison!"

"Melinda, probation is pretty serious. You have to be really careful. If you violate your probation on the last day, you will be subject to prison for the entire sentence. Remember that please?"

Melinda nodded vigorously.

"OK, let's get out of here, shall we?"

Tristan and Melinda joined Kerry, and they walked toward the entrance to the courthouse. Kerry said, "I think we need a celebration dinner. Besides, I bet Melinda hasn't had decent food in weeks!"

"Not since that last dinner we had on Yagan IV."

"God, really? It's been a long haul, hasn't it?"

Tristan said, "It has, but now it's over."

Melinda turned to Tristan and stopped her in the hallway. "Tristan, I'd be a gonner without you. Thank you so much. "

"Melinda, I'm happy to help. There are many people alive that would not be if you hadn't done what you did."

They walked out of the courthouse into chaos. There were literally hundreds of people pressing them and shouting questions at them. Some uniformed officers came to surround them and help, and they made it to a taxi, finally. Kerry told the automated driver where to go.

Melinda asked, "What's all of that?"

Kerry said, "You are famous, sweetheart. I've heard you are a new hero."

Tristan said, "Among some quarters. Some in the government probably won't be happy with what the judge did. That would be those that wanted 'the problem' of TOTC to be eliminated by the aliens."

"That bothers you, love, doesn't it?"

"Yes. And it bothers me that they now have no advocates."

"Are you thinking what I think you're thinking?"

"I have to go back to Dia V, Kerry."

"That's what I thought you were thinking. Why am I not surprised?"

"After hearing all that testimony, it is so obvious. I need to help them find a new home."

"Well, dear heart, if anyone can do it you can. I'm just not at all looking forward to telling my crew we'll be doing shore leave on Dia from now on."

They all laughed.

EPILOGUE

Melinda said, "Captain, jumpgate API ready, we're next in line."

"Thank you, Melinda."

This was her first shift at systems control. She was a little nervous, but it was a routine run, and a routine jumpgate process. She'd learned it and practiced it over and over in simulation. She looked down at her display, and saw the jumpgate systems interface with their systems, and take the ship over for the short time through the gate.

Melinda would never understand jumpgate physics. When the jumpgate to Earth was built, and the Korth arrived, humans learned that most galactic civilizations were thousands of years ahead of them in science and technology. Humans had been able to catch up to many civilizations quickly, but no one except the jumpgate tenders understood the physics of jumpgates. It wasn't because they weren't willing to share. They did. But the consensus was that their brains were just enough different than most, and leaps of understanding were possible for them that just weren't for humans, or most other species.

"Captain, we're through. Jumpgate systems disengaging."

Ainsley said, "We're about an hour out of Shabazz shipyards, Captain."

Melinda had been on the *John Coltrane* for four months. She was enjoying every minute of it. They were stopping at the Shabazz shipyards to get some parts of the ship repaired. Kerry was going to visit her parents, and some other crew were going to hang out on Shabazz. Melinda would be staying with the ship, doing her studies.

The terms of her probation were relatively harsh. When she wasn't working or studying, she had to be at home, or in the presence of Kerry. Home meant on the *John Coltrane*. She and Kerry had agreed that for the most part, for the first year, Melinda would stay on the ship. She wasn't really unhappy. There was plenty to learn and do. She'd become friends with Jeff, who would explain all sorts of things about how the ship worked.

She realized that it wasn't really all that bad a way to spend eight years. And when she was 24, she'd be finished, and she could go her way, and do what she'd like.

Tristan had been waiting for this day for months. The most horrible six months of her life. But it was finally going to be over, for her at least. She had known, two weeks into her six-month self-imposed sentence of being an advocate for the The One True Church, the mission was going to be an utter failure.

The colonists despised her, because she'd been banished, made her way in the world, was a sinner, and was unwilling or unable to conform to their ideals. She was hated by the Galactic officials, representing the most reviled group of Terrans—the ones that had almost jeopardized Earth's place in the galaxy.

Tristan had known some about the hatred people had for the TOTC, and they had mostly been forgotten, until the alien attack. Then, people remembered, and the hatred was fueled by a hundred idiotic rumors that TOTC had been responsible for all of the alien attacks, and the deaths of a million on Rigel. Galactic Central had hardly been aggressive at discounting the rumors.

It had been hopeless, really, and she should have known it. Nothing was going to temper the arrogance of her people, and nothing was going to make anyone at Galactic Central interested in giving them another chance at a colony. Melinda's trial had made it clear that it wasn't colonial autonomy that had fueled the original policy to allow TOTC to stay on Yagan despite the impending attack. It was the hope that the attack would wipe out TOTC entirely and dispense of a bothersome pebble in Galactic Central's shoes.

The current official policy was one of attrition. They were going to remove all unmarried children under 18 from Dia V, and scatter them all over the galaxy, and continue to remove children when they reached the age of one. The rest they would allow to live here until they died. Individuals could petition to leave, but not whole families. This policy wouldn't take so long to reach its obvious conclusion. Her people refused all modern medicine, and this planet was a cold, poisonous pit. They weren't going to live long.

She wasn't going to clue the colonists in that they were about to lose all of their unmarried children under 18. If she did, they would simply marry them all. She had even argued that they should just take everyone under 21, but that was not acceptable to Galactic Central authorities. She had let several people she knew know that there was no hope of another colony, and she could get them off of this planet, but none of them wanted to leave their families.

It was time for her to go. The *John Coltrane* was on its way, and she would be gone. She was sad, a little. It seemed likely that her lifetime would see the final end of TOTC. In a way, they had carried on far too long, anyway.

She packed up her things and puttered around the prefab that had been her home for six months. She didn't expect the colonists to miss her presence. They mostly ignored her anyway.

The primitive system she had chirped. "Message from the *Coltrane*. Shuttle on its way. It should land in about 5 minutes."

She picked up her bags, left the house, closed the door, and walked toward the landing pad. As she walked, she watched the people going about their daily tasks. It was easier for them here, in some ways. They didn't have to build anything or fix anything. There were no domestic animals that could survive on Dia V, nor any crops that could grow. It was a much simpler life, one that Tristan expected would be pretty boring, but they seemed to be adapting.

No one acknowledged her. She didn't expect it. They might wonder when she never came back, but they would be pretty busy dealing with the several hundred officers coming to take their children away. She arrived at the landing pad and looked up to see the shuttle just landing. When it settled down, the door opened, and Kerry and Melinda popped out. She ran to them.

About the Author

Maxwell has been a science fiction fan since he could read. He has written and published poetry, creative nonfiction, and technical writing. He has self-published a number of science fiction novels. Maxwell lives and writes in Northern California.

Connect with him online:

Bluesky: @pearlbear.com

Web: http://author.maxwellpearl.com

**Other Books by Maxwell Pearl
from Echobird Press**

Friends with Wings

ECHOBIRD
PRESS

More by Echobird Press

Fiction
The Alters, a series by Terra Katherine McKeown
Book One – *Chasing Dawn*
Book Two – *Break of Dawn*

Poetry
bones of this land by Kat Heatherington
A Map Without Your Shadow by Kat Heatherington
No Longer Water by Katrina Kaye
bouquet of thorny rose by Sossity Chiricuzio
The Gatekeeper Wears Acrylics by Court Winterborne

Find these and more at www.echobirdpress.com